MW00940212

Praying
at the
Sweetwater Motel

A NOVEL BY

APRIL YOUNG FRITZ

HYPERION BOOKS FOR CHILDREN
NEW YORK

ACKNOWLEDGMENTS

Special thanks to my editor, Donna Bray, for her enthusiasm,
encouragement, and thoughtful editing of this book.
And to all the brave women and children searching
for their safe harbors, I wish you peace.

Printed in the United States of America

First Edition

1 3 5 7 9 10 8 6 4 2

The text for this book is set in 13 point Horley.

Library of Congress Cataloging-in-Publication data on file

ISBN 0-7868-1864-6

Visit www.hyperionchildrensbooks.com

For my mother,
June Kelly Young,
my first reader

In memory of my sister,
Ellen Young—
I miss you

Contents

Praying
at the
Sweetwater Motel

★

Hello, God, it's me, Sarah Jane Otis. You haven't seen me in church lately, but that's because Mama's given up on you. She says no one's going to answer our prayers, so why bother? Please don't be mad at her. She's just feeling kind of hopeless lately. I still believe you'll help us, so from now on, I'll do the praying for my whole family. Here goes. Please don't let my daddy come home drunk again tonight. I know I always ask you for the same thing, but the last time we were in church, Mr. Tucker announced that he'd seen the light and given up drinking. Since my daddy still comes home too drunk to get his car into the garage, I thought maybe you got someone else's prayer mixed up with mine. I live at 852 Sherman Avenue in the white house with the blue shutters that need painting. I share a room with my sister, Alice, but I am the one doing all the serious praying. She is only four and doesn't understand what's going on. Thank you for listening. Any help will be appreciated. Amen.

CHAPTER 1

Red Boots

THE DAY we left, Mama woke me a few hours before dawn. She leaned down, touched her lips to my forehead, and whispered, "Time to go, Sarah Jane."

I nuzzled against her warm skin and smelled the sweetness of her bath powder.

"We're leaving now," she said. "Don't dawdle."

I rolled over in my bed to peer across at my sister, Alice, sound asleep, wrapped like an eggroll in her Barbie bedspread, her thumb jammed in her mouth.

Mama looked beautiful that night, her long blond hair tied back with a ribbon. She wore her pink cotton sundress, her shoulders covered by a baby-blue cardigan embroidered with pink roses. I noticed she had on her Keds instead of the white leather ballet slippers she usually wore with that outfit.

"Better for driving," she told me when she saw me looking at her feet. Her straw satchel, the one she bought on our vacation at Virginia Beach, sat on the floor, its sides bulging with her treasures.

The moon-shaped night-light washed the walls with a soft glow. I studied my room, with its wallpaper border of horses galloping across a pasture, the tieback curtains Mama sewed on her old Singer, and the bookcases filled with favorite stories. The rocker where my baby sister and I once sat crushed against Mama as she read to us sat still and empty in the corner.

I held the image in my mind, willing it to stay in place the way I hold Coca-Cola in my mouth when I come to the bottom of the glass, believing if I savor the last drops, later I'll be able to sweep my tongue against the roof of my mouth and taste the sweetness once more.

Mama unwrapped Alice from her bedspread.

Alice whimpered, caught in the hazy place between sleep and wakefulness.

"We need to hurry," Mama said as she perched on the edge of the bed, peeling Alice's nightgown over her head, replacing it with a T-shirt. Alice wiggled as Mama tugged white shorts over her skinny legs, snapping the elastic waistband in place.

I removed my own nightgown and tossed it on the floor. Underneath, I was already dressed in my red tank top with the purple stripes and denim shorts soft from wear. I pulled on a pair of white tube socks and the red cowboy boots my daddy gave me for my birthday in March. He said they were real cowboy boots from Texas, hand-tooled with oak leaves and acorns, and heels thick enough to hang on to stirrups no matter how wild the horse.

I knew he felt bad because he couldn't afford to buy me the horse I wanted. *Next year*, he promised, next year I'd have my horse. Mama said sometimes Daddy made promises he couldn't keep.

It would have broken my heart to leave the

red boots behind. Mama agreed it was smart to wear them on our trip since they'd take up the space of three pairs of shoes in my suitcase; leaving home under special circumstances forced us to make hard decisions about what was really important, what we couldn't live without.

Four-year-old Alice, eight years younger than me and a miniature version of Mama, was not included in the planning of our *adventure*, as Mama referred to the trip that would take us far from the only home I had ever known. Alice could not be trusted to keep our secret even if she crossed her heart and hoped to die that she wouldn't tell a single soul, especially our Daddy.

The week before we ran away, Mama settled Alice on the living room couch with her blankie and a bag of chocolate-chip cookies. She popped a video into the VCR, ensuring we'd have some peace and quiet to make our plans.

I brewed a pot of tea, and we sipped from china cups usually saved for company as we made a list of what to take. Mama had already gone to the school and retrieved copies of my school records. She put them into a special folder, along with our birth certificates and the medical records we might need.

"Don't forget to write down 'Cat food for Mabel.'"

I added it to the list, which grew so long, I worried we might have trouble fitting everything into our car.

I wished we could rent a giant truck so we wouldn't have to leave anything behind. Mama said renting a truck would leave a paper trail that would lead Daddy to us.

She hid the folder and the lists I made in the car beneath the spare tire. She'd been cutting coupons for months to use at the grocery store and putting aside the money she saved. The thick stack of bills waited in an envelope taped to the bottom of my dresser drawer.

After months of anticipation, we were finally putting our plans into action. It made me feel important, being included, like the time Mama said I could stay in the living room when the social worker came, after Daddy beat her real bad and she had to go to the hospital for stitches.

"He may kill you the next time," the social

worker warned Mama. "I wish you'd file a police report against him. He should be in jail for what he did to you."

The social worker's name was Kim, and she seemed to forget about me as I sat cross-legged in front of the TV watching *I Love Lucy* with the sound turned down. She had silky blond hair like Mama's, and skin so perfect I couldn't imagine anyone covering it with angry purple bruises.

Mama was afraid to send Daddy to jail. And I think she was ashamed for people to find out what went on inside our house, as if she was to blame. It made me wonder if I might be at fault for making Daddy angry.

Mama hid the bruises on her arms under long-sleeved blouses and the ones on her face with pancake makeup. If she got a black eye, she wore sunglasses, even on rainy days. When I told her it looked strange for her to wear sunglasses when there was no sun, she said maybe people would think she was a movie star.

"Let's go," said Mama, rousing me from my reverie. I carted her satchel through the dark house, careful not to let it bump against a wall and sound a warning.

Mama carried Alice pressed against the length of her. In the dim hallway it was difficult to see where one began and the other ended, the way it was before Alice was born. We eased ourselves out the front door, with me inching the screen door closed for fear the slightest sound might wake our daddy, asleep in the back bedroom.

"Hush now," Mama whispered to Alice when she complained she had to pee. "You can go at the Dunkin' Donuts. I'll buy you some Munchkins if you're good. Be a quiet little mouse for Mama."

Daddy's Buick straddled the driveway, its right tires on the lawn. Just hours before, too keyed-up to sleep, I'd kept watch from my bedroom window. He came home past midnight and staggered to the house. I heard him cussing a stream of words that didn't amount to a sentence when he couldn't get his key to work the lock. Mama let him in and helped him into bed. She couldn't allow him to fall asleep on the couch and ruin our plans.

Once outside, Mama set Alice on the curb. She walked over to the Buick, the driver's door left ajar, reached in, and pulled the knob for the headlights.

"A dead battery will buy us more time," she said.

Our other car, an old Chevy wagon, was nowhere to be seen. Mama'd stashed it while Daddy was out, knowing he'd think she'd parked it in the garage. Daddy never attempted to park his car in the garage after a night of drinking; the one time he had, he crumpled the right fender and ripped a piece of aluminum siding from the house.

Mama struggled with Alice, who had managed to rewrap herself toga-style in her bedspread.

"Where's Mabel?" I asked. I'd been so scared Daddy would wake up that I'd forgotten about our cat.

"Mabel's already in the car, baby girl, probably having a hissy fit. Now, come on before your daddy wakes up and finds us gone."

I hung back, stealing one last look at our

house. It seemed sad, with its overgrown lawn and the porch light that hung away from its mooring by a wire.

The other houses on the street stood dark, the Snells, the Robinsons, and the Willies asleep in their beds. Tomorrow they would gather on their lawns and talk about us. They would invite Daddy to eat supper on their patios, and between bites of ribs and potato salad he would ask them what he had done to deserve this. Hadn't he been a good provider? Did he ever cheat or mess around with other women? And Mrs. Willie would touch her pouf of black hair and say, "Why no, Darryl," because she had always been sweet on my daddy.

The neighbors would believe whatever he told them, because Mama mostly kept her troubles to herself. Except for confiding in the social worker and her best friend, Nancy Pitcher, she kept our secrets locked inside her and told me to do the same.

I have to make this quick, God, because I am trying to keep up with Mama, and it's hard to pray and run at the same time. You see, I haven't been telling you the whole truth about Mama's accidents. Daddy's been beating on her, and we have to leave and go someplace safe. Please don't let him wake up until you can see our taillights moving along the highway. At least let us get a head start. Mama's telling me to get a move on, so bye for now.

CHAPTER 2

Secrets

EVEN THOUGH Mama'd told me to keep our secret to ourselves, I figured it was okay to tell God. I prayed every day for Daddy to stay sober and for the fighting to stop.

I wanted to stay in our house and sleep in my own room. I'd miss having dinner every Sunday at Grandma Emma's and riding her old quarter horse, Pete.

I'd planned on starting seventh grade at the new middle school with my best friend, Marion. We liked to go to the movies and hang out at her house. I never heard her parents raise their voices to each other. Mama said people acted different when they had company. She said every family had its problems.

I don't remember it being so bad when I was little, and I can't put my finger on the exact moment when it changed. It's not as if Daddy was nice one day and mean the next. The change in him came gradually, the way the water in our birdbath turns from warm to cool and then to ice, one layer at a time.

Mama and Daddy didn't always fight. I remember when Daddy was happy. He owned his own service station in town, and he'd wave to me when I passed his place on the school bus. When he worked late to fix a car for someone who needed it done right away, Mama packed up a picnic dinner, and the four of us ate at the big desk in his office.

Mama would whisper, "Hurry home," and give him a big, sloppy kiss, while Alice and I chose candy from the display case.

Mama claimed she never saw a man work so hard, that he wasn't to blame for the business failing. Once the interstate got rerouted, business got slow. Half the stores in town stood empty, and the few customers who asked my daddy to fix their cars couldn't always pay.

Most of the fights between Mama and Daddy seemed to be about money. Like the time last October, Mama got Alice and me clothes at the Nearly New thrift shop and Daddy yelled at her, saying she did it on purpose to shame him for not being a better provider. That's when she screamed right back, telling him he was a fool to buy the service station in the first place.

"I like these clothes, Daddy," I told him, modeling the outfit so he could see how nice I looked. But in the morning I found the shirt and pants from the Nearly New stuffed in the garbage pail.

The week before Thanksgiving he taped a FOR SALE sign in the window of the service station. It hung there for three months until the red letters faded to pink and the tape dried up, letting the sign fall to the floor.

The man at the bank called to say he was sorry, but since my daddy couldn't pay the mortgage on the service station and it didn't look like there were any buyers, the bank had no choice but to foreclose on the property.

Mama suggested she could get a job at the supermarket or wait tables, but that only made Daddy angrier. He said no wife of his was going to work.

On Easter Sunday, the day before the bank held an auction to sell the service station to the highest bidder, Daddy started big-time drinking. I suspect he'd been fantasizing that he'd win the lottery or something and be able to buy his place back.

After dinner, he said we should take a look around the place one more time. He still had a key to the side door. At first he walked around real quiet, touching his desk, the walls, tapping his foot against the car lift.

Mama held my hand. A tremor passed from her to me. Fear darkened her eyes. I followed her line of vision in time to see Daddy pick up a tire iron propped against the wall.

He smashed the windows first. Then he went after the walls, punching holes with the tire iron and yanking hard enough to split them open until they looked like the bellies of gutted deer, their insides spilling onto the floor.

Mama shielded Alice and me with her body as we huddled beneath the desk, the same desk where we'd once eaten picnic suppers, and spoken in our soft indoor voices.

Mama told Daddy he was lucky no one ever found out what he'd done or he would have gone to jail. She told Alice a pack of lies, convinced her that Daddy had demolished everything so someone could redecorate.

I still had to pass the service station each day on the bus. It made me sad to see it boarded up. Once I spotted Daddy sitting by the gas pumps, his head buried in his hands.

Periods of calm gave me hope. Like when Daddy got a job at the plant where they make cars, and he earned enough money so Mama could pay the bills.

We'd eat hot dogs and beans on Sunday nights and play Monopoly in front of the TV. Daddy stopped drinking so much, and he'd put Alice to bed and read her stories until she fell asleep.

Some nights, after I cleared the table, I'd spy on Mama from the tree house in our backyard.

She'd wash dishes at the sink in our yellow kitchen, her slender arms encased in rubber gloves the color of butter, gloves so sleek that from a distance they might have been the ones ladies wore to the opera.

I'd move my own mouth to mimic her red lips as she sang along with the radio. Framed by the window and illuminated by the soft glow of the kitchen light, she resembled a work of art.

Just when I thought things had changed, Daddy started having problems at work. He said his boss was a jerk and that he hated working on a production line, attaching doors to cars, hour after hour, day after day, until he thought he'd go out of his mind.

"I like to be my own boss!" he shouted, as he pounded his fist on the kitchen table, hard enough to make the glasses jump.

Since he couldn't be the boss, he did the next-best thing and began to boss Mama. He picked on her about the teeniest things, telling her she didn't set the table right or that she wore too much makeup and dressed too sexy.

The more he drank, the more things got

broken. Mama covered the holes he punched into the walls with our artwork. I hid anything breakable that I cared about.

I'd wanted to believe Mama when she told me her bruises came from slipping on the kitchen floor, or hitting her head on the doorjamb when she got up in the middle of the night to go to the bathroom.

But one day I caught her sobbing her eyes out. I'd come inside for a drink of water, and there she stood leaning against the wall, her body shaking with her fear. I thought maybe someone had died.

I patted her back the way you comfort a baby. She turned and threw her arms around me. "Oh, Sarah Jane," she said, "what am I going to do?"

That's when she told me Daddy'd been the one putting the bruises on her. I didn't know what to do anymore than she did, so I began to pray every morning and night and sometimes in the middle of the day. Once I even caught myself praying out loud at school.

I didn't tell the whole truth because I didn't want God to think poorly about my daddy. I prayed for Mama to stop having so many "accidents."

Then it happened. That night in May, the screaming got so bad I couldn't shut it out with two pillows wrapped around my ears. The noise woke Alice too, but I told her it was the TV on too loud and to go back to sleep.

Daddy stood over Mama in the kitchen as she lay against an overturned chair, her nose bleeding, her eyes already swelling into purple plums.

"Get back to bed, Sarah Jane," she pleaded.

The wind howled outside. We stood apart on the black-and-white tiled floor of the kitchen of our little house, chess pieces daring each other to make the next move. Hailstones pelted the windows and bounced off our roof. A man on the radio announced tornado sightings. The town siren shrieked a warning. We were trapped.

Mama never would have left to save herself. She kept hoping the mean Daddy would change back to the nice one. That if she kept the house clean, made his favorite meals, and if we were quiet while he read his paper, and if, if, if . . .

That night when I appeared in the kitchen to

defend her, she knew I had crossed with her into enemy territory. It didn't matter that I resembled Daddy, with his thick brown hair and fierce black eyes—all he saw was a traitor.

"Stop hitting her!" I screamed at him.

Daddy lurched toward me, his face red and bloated, the stink of beer hot on his breath. I backed up until I felt the wall against my back. His large meaty hand cut the air, catching the side of my face. My head jerked away with the force of the blow, knocking me against the door-jamb, splitting the skin over my cheekbone.

Mama charged at Daddy with a kitchen chair, poking him with the legs like a lion tamer trying to control a ferocious beast. "Touch her again and I will kill you!" she screamed at him.

I'd never seen her so angry, her face contorted, her arms moving like pistons as she jabbed at him.

"Not if I kill you first!" he yelled, yanking the chair from her hands and throwing it across the room.

"Run, Sarah Jane!" Mama picked up the

toaster and aimed it at Daddy. It bounced against his forehead, stunning him long enough for us to get to my bedroom.

Alice woke as we barreled through the door. Mama slammed it shut and locked it.

"Help me with this," she said. We barricaded the door with my dresser.

"I'm scared," said Alice.

I didn't know if she was scared because she'd heard Mama's screaming or because of the storm. "I'll turn on a light."

I switched on the lamp on her bedside table, and then huddled with her under the covers. Mama sat on the floor, her back pressed against the dresser.

The doorknob rattled. "Open the door!" Daddy shouted as he pounded on the door hard enough to cause the dresser to vibrate.

Mama dug in her heels. "Go away."

"This is my house. I'm not going anywhere."

"Then we'll leave!" Mama screamed at him. She looked over at me. The fury in her eyes told me she'd had enough.

"I'll never let you leave me. Just try and see

what happens. No matter where you go, I'll find you and drag you back by your hair."

A loud crack pierced the air outside. Something hit the roof. I peered out the window. An uprooted tree rested against the house.

I turned to face Mama and Alice. "It's the big tree. It came right out of the ground."

Alice stared at me. "Sarah Jane, you're bleeding."

I ran to the mirror, afraid to look. Blood seeped from my cheek. It stung when I touched it.

"We need to get that fixed." Mama told me to press a clean sock against it to stop the bleeding.

Mama abandoned her post to help Alice into a sweater and some shoes. I put on some clothes over my pajamas and slipped into a pair of flip-flops.

Mama eased open my bedroom window. She helped me over the sill and passed Alice to me before she climbed out herself.

We clung to each other as we cut through our neighbors' yards to get to Grandma Emma's house. The wind pushed against us one minute and propelled us the next. I don't know what I feared most, being sucked up by a twister or dragged home and dealt with by my daddy. Either one could be deadly.

We got to Grandma Emma's and pounded on her kitchen door. The light came on. The door flew open. She gaped at the three of us standing there on her back stoop, wind-whipped and crying.

"Oh, my darlings," was all she said. She swept us into her warm kitchen and gathered us in her arms.

Grandma Emma settled Alice in her big bed and got antiseptic and Band-Aids for me. Mama sat me on the couch. Tears streamed down her face and her hands shook as she fixed my cut with a butterfly bandage.

"Sarah Jane, this has to be our secret. If anyone asks what happened to your face, tell them you fell off your bike."

Grandma Emma wanted to call the police and let them lock Daddy away where he couldn't hurt us anymore, but Mama was afraid he'd get out and do worse.

We returned home the next morning. Daddy acted remorseful and seemed to believe us when we said we forgave him. Mama said we had to bide our time and to lie if need be to keep Daddy from suspecting we were making plans to leave. For three months we planned our escape.

The night we left, I stood close to Mama, fingering the scar on my cheekbone, its raised pink edge the shape of a crescent moon.

I wanted to run back inside the house, nail the dresser to my bedroom door, and lock out the world. If only I could stay there, with my horse wallpaper, the rocking chair, and my books, I'd be safe. If only I could stay.

Please, God, can you send us a miracle before it's too late? I don't want to leave home. It's not fair. Can't you do something, put a spell on Daddy and change him back to the way he used to be? Send me a sign Anything.

CHAPTER 3
On the Road

OUR CAR STOOD parked in front of Nancy Pitcher's house. As soon as Nancy spotted us, she jumped up from the porch steps and tossed her cigarette on the lawn. She reminded me of a football player, all shoulders and a big head made even larger with her teased-up red hair.

"I filled the car with gas and had the oil checked. Put air in the tires too."

Seeing our car stuffed to its roof with piles of Alice's baby dolls, the small TV from the kitchen, and Mama's favorite fern crammed into the way-back made our leaving real. I began to cry, and that set Alice to wailing.

Nancy took Alice into the house and let her use the toilet and got her a glass of water. The whole time they were inside, Mama watched the street for Daddy. I couldn't take my eyes off my beautiful purple bike leaning up against Nancy's carport. Her little girl Justine would be riding it up and down the sidewalk this summer; she was too young to take it in the street.

The screen door swung open and Mama reached for Alice, pulling her close and kissing the top of her head as if she had been gone a long time. Nancy swiped at her eyes and heaved a sigh.

"You girls be good for your mama," she said, and then hugged all of us.

For once Alice didn't pitch a fit and insist on sitting in front. Mama arranged her in the back on her booster seat with a pillow behind her head and a couple of My Little Ponies in her lap. She told Alice she could be in charge of Mabel, who meowed from inside her carrier.

I got to sit up front and be copilot. Nancy leaned into the car and gave Mama one final hug. She pressed a wad of folded money into her hand

and passed a bag filled with sandwiches, fruit, and soda pops to me.

"There's a sack of chocolate Kisses in there. Don't eat them all at once." Nancy backed away from the car. "I wish I knew where you were going, so I could write."

"It's better this way," said Mama. She held out her hand, her pink iridescent nails glowing under the streetlight. "I'll miss you," she said to Nancy.

"I'll miss you too," Nancy said. Her mouth twisted with a sob. She turned and ran into her house, letting the door slap shut behind her.

We passed Grandma Emma's house on our way out of town. Mama flicked the car lights off and on. Grandma Emma blew us kisses from where she stood on her front porch, proud and tall, a brave soldier. I leaned from the car window and caught her kisses with my hands. We'd said our good-byes the day before. Mama promised to call her when it was safe.

We never did stop at Dunkin' Donuts like Mama promised. Alice fell asleep two blocks from Nancy's, and Mama said, "Better to let sleeping dogs lie," so we headed onto the ramp to the interstate. When we came to the split we took the one that said NORTH.

"I thought we'd be going to Florida, Mama. Every time we went there on vacation, you always said that's where you'd like to live. I remember you saying to Daddy, 'Darryl, Florida is the place for me.'"

Mama didn't answer right away. She asked me to open her a Coke and to pass her a Salem from the pack in the glove compartment. It was only after she finished half her pop and got her cigarette going to a hard burn that she let me in on her plans.

"I'm hoping that's what he'll think and he'll look for us there." She smiled at me. "Sarah Jane, we're going to Ohio. Take a look at that magazine under the seat, see where I got it marked?"

I pulled a copy of *Family Circle* from under my seat and read the article entitled "Ohio, the Heart of it All." "It's got a big zoo," I said. I wondered if I would make any friends there. Not that I had that many to speak of in Georgia, but when you come right down to it, all you need is one.

One true friend like Marion who won't care if you have crooked teeth because you can't afford braces and who invites you for sleepovers at her house even if you can't pay her back. I hoped Marion would forgive me for not saying good-bye.

We drove all night, through a hard rain that caused other people to pull off the road to wait it out. Mama said we couldn't spare the time, that every mile between us and Daddy was like buying another insurance policy. Alice slept, perspiration on her forehead turning her bangs to ringlets. I sucked on Hershey's Kisses until I couldn't stand the taste. Ordinarily Mama would have been on me about rotting my teeth, but that night we were two women on a mission.

Mama said this once we could splurge on a real motel, not a no-name one with rough sheets. We stopped at first light at a Day's Inn, parking our car at the back of the lot, so it couldn't be seen from the road. Our room had two double beds and a bathroom with a coffeemaker built into the wall. The balcony overlooked an indoor swimming pool with an arched glass roof that reminded me of a cathedral.

Mama and I made an Alice sandwich on the bed, with her sleeping in between us, her tiny legs beating against me as she ran away from something in her sleep. It seemed a shame to let the extra bed go to waste, but Mama said she needed to feel us next to her or she wouldn't sleep a wink.

I woke a little past noon, the room as dark as a cave except for a sliver of light where the draperies didn't quite close. Mama sat in a chair by the door smoking a cigarette and sipping a cup of coffee she had made in the little pot in the bathroom. Mabel perched on the TV set watching over us.

The manager said we could stay past checkout because we'd gotten in so late. We ate leftover peanut-butter-and-jelly sandwiches for breakfast. Mama seemed jittery and said she couldn't eat a bite.

"Are you ever going to wear shoes again?" she asked me when I pulled on my red boots, as she stood over Alice, running a brush through her tangled hair.

"Yes, ma'am," I told her. "When my feet grow so long the boots pinch my toes."

Even then, I'd hide the boots from Alice. She was welcome to my outgrown sneakers and my white moccasins with the Indian beads; the red boots were mine as long as I had breath in my body.

For the rest of the trip I sat with my feet propped up on the dashboard, the road atlas spread open across my legs, ready to help Mama with directions. When I flipped the pages to a map of the whole United States, I noticed that Ohio did look like a heart. Maybe things would be different there. Mama would find us a place with a yellow kitchen where she'd wash dishes in the sunlight and sing along with the radio. I'd make friends who could sleep over, and sometimes I'd let Alice stay up and watch videos with us.

Then one night, like a magic trick that happens when you look away, I would sleep all the way through till morning.

Dear God, it's me again, Sarah Jane Otis. I wanted to ask you to watch over my daddy. I'm not saying I'm not still angry with him, because I am. What he did was wrong. But I don't want anything bad to happen to him or for him to go to jail. He never did stop drinking. I don't blame you, or anything. Mama told me Daddy's drinking would try the patience of a saint, which I figured is what happened and why you gave up on him. I still need your help. When he wakes up and finds us gone, he is going to be as riled up as the day the bank took his business. Please don't let him find us. If he does, he will hurt Mama real bad. We'll be the ones in the beat-up car with the missing hubcap.

CHAPTER 4

No Room at the Inn

AS WE DROVE through Kentucky, I couldn't help wondering about Daddy. I imagined him waking up in our little house, the kitchen quiet without the sounds of Mama making breakfast and Alice's cartoons on TV. What was he thinking that exact moment he realized we were gone? Was he sad or was he angry?

We'd cut him from our lives with one swift motion just as Mama had chopped the sickly branch from the red maple in our backyard. I'd begged her not to do it. We'd hung our swing from that limb. Mama said if we didn't remove it, the whole tree would die.

"Quit looking for him," Mama said when I

35

craned my neck to see out the back window, most of the view blocked by our stuff piled high. "Don't you worry, we got enough of a head start."

I couldn't tell her what I was thinking, that I still prayed for a miracle and half-hoped Daddy would catch up to us and promise to quit drinking and be nice the way he used to be.

Alice still didn't understand the truth, that we were running away from home. She sat in the back of the car playing happily with the paper dolls Mama had bought her for the trip, changing their clothes more times than I could count.

"Lookie here, Sarah Jane," she said in her high-pitched voice every time she put a new outfit on one of the dolls, careful to fold the tabs just so.

I oohed and aahed to keep her satisfied, which was my job. Mama said she had to concentrate on the road and make plans for our future. She sipped coffee, hot and steamy from a thermos cup that I refilled without spilling a drop.

"I am thinking deep thoughts," she said to

me whenever I tried to engage her in conversation. Then she'd smile at me and ask, "Don't you hear the wheels spinning in Mama's head? They're going a hundred miles a minute trying to figure out what to do."

"Don't you know? I thought you'd been planning things for months."

"You can't be too careful when it comes to your daddy. I swear, the man could read my mind. It's best if we wing it for a while."

"I guess you're right, but—"

"No buts about it, Sarah Jane. Trust me on this. Just think of this as an adventure, baby girl. Things will settle down soon enough." She lit another cigarette, ending the conversation.

Adventures were for pirates and people who flew into outer space. I liked everything to be the same. Why, I could eat grilled-cheese sandwiches for lunch every day for the rest of my life.

An adventure had seemed like a good idea as we planned our escape, but not knowing what was going to happen was scary. Where would we live? Would I ever have another friend?

We stopped for dinner at one of those big

truck stops where you can buy a hot shower for a dollar and even wash your clothes. I walked Mabel on the leash we had bought just for the trip. She did her business in a sandy area behind some bushes. The day had cooled down enough so it was okay to leave her in the car with a bowl of food and some fresh water.

"We're having an adventure, Mabel," I told her before shutting the door to her crate. "It's going to be okay."

The air-conditioning in the truck stop raised goose bumps on my arms. Mama offered me her sweater. I wore it the way she did, slipped over my shoulders.

She ordered hamburgers, fries, and chocolate milk for Alice and me, a small salad and coffee for herself. We ate in a booth near an exit door.

Trucks and cars on the interstate whizzed by in the distance. Everybody seemed to know where they were going.

I imagined Daddy's Buick appearing on the horizon and pictured him climbing out of his car, still wearing his bowling shirt. He'd stare at us through the plate-glass window, and before we could make a run for it, he'd stand between Mama and the door and beg her to forgive him. In my daydream, he'd smile and promise everything would be different, that he was a changed man and he would sooner cut off his hand than strike Mama or me again, if only we would come home.

Daddy didn't find us, not that day at least. And I didn't witness any miracles. We finished our meals and used the bathroom. Mama ran a comb through her hair and slicked pink lipstick across her mouth. I wondered when Mama slept. She looked worn out.

"It's the light in here," she said when she caught me staring at her face in the mirrored wall over the sinks. "It gives everybody dark circles under their eyes."

Mama's hand shook as she lit up a cigarette outside the restaurant. "Don't start on me about smoking." She turned her back to take a last draw on her cigarette before she stubbed it out in an ashtray by the door. "After we're safe," she whispered to me so Alice wouldn't hear. "I'll quit then, I promise."

We crossed the Ohio River from Kentucky into Ohio. Streaks of orange and pink painted the sky. I held the map open for Mama and gazed down at the river below. The river divided the life we left behind from the life that lay ahead. This scared and thrilled me at the same time.

It was almost midnight when Mama pulled off the road so we could get our bearings. "This is where we are," she said, pointing to a highway on the map that ran in a circle around Columbus, Ohio.

We drove east, then north, moving counterclockwise, passing towns called Reynoldsburg, New Albany, and Westerville.

"When are we going to stop?" I asked. Alice slept contentedly, her blankie draped over her head. I longed for a real bed.

"Just say the word, baby girl. I'm so tired I could sleep on a sidewalk." Mama drained the last of the coffee. "We're due north of Columbus. If we don't pull off this highway soon, we're going to end up where we started. Going around in circles, so to speak. Like my life."

I looked up and to see a large green sign suspended above us, the word DUBLIN spelled out in big white letters.

"Look, Mama, Dublin, like in Ireland."

She threw back her head and laughed. "I do believe we've been driving so long, we've crossed the ocean."

"Let's stop here." Dublin made me think of pretty cottages and horses grazing in green fields.

We turned off the main road, onto a narrow, curvy exit that dropped us off in the middle of a small town, its main street lined on either side with low brick buildings, and a supermarket still lit up.

Alice woke when Mama stopped the car under a canopy in front of the office of a two-story brick motel. "Stay here with Sarah Jane. Mama'll be right back."

Lightning flashed across the sky. At the first sound of thunder Alice began to whimper. I climbed in the back to shush her. Huddled in the dark, we waited for Mama to return. Fingers of rain moving sideways dashed against our car, as if they wanted inside in the worst way.

Mama was gone a long time and by the look on her face when she came back to the car, she was not happy.

"There's no room at the inn," she said, and started the engine before I had a chance to take my place next to her in the front.

"We can try somewhere else. Look, there's one right across the street." I pointed to a hotel sign.

"Sarah Jane, why do you think I was gone so long? The girl at the desk told me there's some kind of convention in town and all the nearby hotels are full. She even called around for me, but no one's got a room."

I knew that if I cried, Alice would start, and Mama looked like she was out of patience. "Where are we going?"

"I'm about to fall asleep at the wheel, so we'd better stay here for the night."

"But you said there aren't any rooms."

Mama glared at me before putting the car in gear and driving around to the back of the motel. She pulled into an empty spot between a van and a truck. "We'll be okay here for the night."

Just when I thought things couldn't get worse, they did. "You mean we're going to sleep in the parking lot?"

"Just for tonight. Pretend we're camping." The rain had eased to a mist. She climbed out of the car, turned her back to me, and lit up a cigarette.

I rolled down the window to talk to her. "When we go camping we take sleeping bags and a tent."

"Don't be contrary, Sarah Jane."

"What if someone sees us? Won't we get in trouble?"

"The light over here is burned out and most everybody's tucked in bed by now."

I wished she hadn't said that. At that moment, I would have given anything for a real bed to sleep in. "I have to pee."

"Go squat in the grass over there."

"Mama!"

"Oh, all right, come on, then. And get Sister out of the car while you're at it." She squashed out her cigarette with the toe of her shoe.

The skies opened up again. Mama sprinted

across the parking lot with Alice in her arms. She paused at the door, and whispered to me to hold my head high and pretend that we owned the place.

The girl behind the front desk chatted on the phone. She didn't seem to care that a tired-looking woman and two stinky kids straggled across the lobby dripping water on the nice red-and-gold carpet without so much as a "Hey."

Mama set Alice down and we filed into the ladies' room. After we'd all gone to the bathroom and washed our hands, I rinsed my mouth as best I could at the sink, wishing I'd thought to bring in my toothbrush.

"Gee whiz, Sarah Jane, your teeth can survive one night without a brushing. Let's get back to the car before somebody breaks a window and steals our stuff."

Now I'd never get a wink of sleep, worrying someone would smash out a window and reach into where we slept.

Mama rolled her eyes at me. "Don't let that imagination of yours run wild. No one will bother us."

I walked Mabel while Mama settled Alice on

the backseat. There wasn't room for me to share the space with Alice, so I had to make do in front with a pillow and a blanket.

"This is uncomfortable. I can't sleep sitting up."

Mama leaned her pillow against her window. "Pretend you're on an airplane. People sleep on airplanes all the time."

I pulled the blanket up to my chin and closed my eyes. Somewhere at the other end of the parking lot, a car door slammed. I watched a man and woman holding hands run through the rain toward the motel. They probably had a room to go to, with a big bed, soft sheets, and four pillows. They had no idea how lucky they were.

God, I am in a grumpy mood this morning, so don't take what I am going to say personally. Have I been reciting the wrong prayer? Do I have to be more specific when I pray? Like ask for a real bed to sleep in instead of the front seat of a car? Please let us find a place to stay with soft beds and a clean bathroom. I have a crick in my neck, and Alice is starting to stink.

CHAPTER 5

The Sweetwater Motel

I T WAS STILL raining in the morning. I walked Mabel, put her back in her crate, and gave her some food and water. The last time we'd taken her to the vet, he said she was overweight. If she didn't get more exercise, she was going to explode. She was beginning to resemble a fur volleyball.

Alice woke up screaming for food. We'd eaten the last of the peanut-butter-and-jelly sandwiches the day before.

"Follow me and do what I do," Mama told me as we dashed through the parking lot.

Instead of taking us to the ladies' room, Mama led us down a hallway with signs and arrows that said TO POOL.

"We can clean up in the locker room," she said as she handed me a bag with our tooth-brushes and a comb for our hair.

After we got ourselves presentable, Mama settled Alice at a table in a room at the back of the lobby, near a buffet table. People stood in line heaping food on white china plates.

The smell of bacon made my mouth water. Mama filled a plate with pancakes, eggs, and bacon and placed it in front of me. "Share this with Alice. I'll be right back."

I watched as she got herself a mug of black coffee and a piece of toast. The place was crowded. A few people poured coffee into Styrofoam cups and headed out the door. Some went back for seconds of everything.

"Is this one of those 'all you can eat' buf-fets?" I asked Mama. "Is it expensive?"

She pointed to a sign on a stand by the door-way: COMPLIMENTARY BREAKFAST BUFFET.

"What does that mean?"

"It means it's free. The breakfast comes with the room."

"But we don't have room."

Mama pressed her lips together. "Well, that's not my fault. We would have had a room if they weren't all full. So eat up."

I leaned close so no one would hear. "But isn't this stealing?"

She sighed and pointed at the buffet table. "Do you see how much food they have? I'll bet you a million dollars they'll be throwing half of it away. So stop acting like I'm a criminal and eat your eggs."

I did as she said. I'd been praying for a miracle, maybe this was a small one. A free breakfast buffet. After Alice had her fill, I finished every scrap on the plate, then went back for seconds. Mama drank two cups of coffee and ate toast with grape jelly.

After we finished eating, we ran through the rain again to our car. Mama put Alice in her seat and passed a bit of bacon to Mabel.

She turned to me. "Last night that girl at the front desk told me about a little place a few miles out of town. She said it's not the Ritz, but it's clean. I was too tired to drive around any more in that storm, but maybe we can find it today."

I climbed into the backseat to get my sweater. "I want to sit up front," said Alice. She pinched me to make her point.

"Hey, stop that." I pushed her little fingers away from my middle and opened the last box of juice, holding it for her as she sipped from the straw.

"She didn't get much sleep last night," said Mama, as usual making excuses for Alice's bad behavior.

As soon as Mama pulled out of the parking lot onto the road, Alice's eyes closed and she fell back to sleep, still sucking on the straw, the way she had when she was a baby and she fell asleep sucking on a baby bottle.

"We're supposed to take a left at the fourth light." The road took us past a shopping center. "This doesn't look like a place for a motel. I hope that girl wasn't sending us on a wild-goose chase."

The storm clouds and rain made the sky as dark as night. "Is that it?" I pointed to a stone building hugging the curve of the road.

Mama shook her head, looking more worried

by the minute. "No, that's a restaurant. See the sign?"

I was so disappointed I almost missed seeing the entrance to the Columbus Zoo. "Look, Mama, it's the zoo."

"Don't bother me now." She took her foot off the gas and the car slowed to a crawl. "How can I concentrate on finding this place with you jabbering in my ear?"

She pulled the car off to the side of the road, shifted it into park, and rested her head on the steering wheel.

"Are you okay, Mama?"

She waved her hand. Her head remained still. "I just need a minute to think." Her voice came out in a whisper; she wasn't mad at me anymore.

"Okay, I got it." She raised her head with a jerk. "That girl at the motel said if we passed the zoo, we'd have gone too far. We should have turned left onto a bridge at that restaurant you spotted."

I felt proud of myself for noticing the restaurant and pointing it out to Mama. As if I'd saved the day.

She swung the car in a U-turn and we headed back in the other direction. The lighted bridge carried us across a river and deposited us in a spot with a restaurant on our left and a market on the right.

"It should be up the road a piece," said Mama. She turned right at a blinking light.

"What's this place called?"

"The Sweetwater Motel. Be on the lookout for it."

I was imagining us spending another night sleeping in our car when I spied it. The Sweetwater Motel sat back from the road, its sign almost invisible behind the rain, now coming down hard as nails.

"There it is. Over there, Mama."

She slammed on the brakes, and the car skidded to a stop next to a beat-up pickup truck. I counted five cars lined up in front of the L-shaped building, but there was no sign of a living soul.

I turned Mama's wrist so I could read her watch. Half past eight.

"Aren't you going in?" I looked over at Mama,

who was fishing in her purse for her cigarettes.

"Give me a minute, will you? Just give me a darned second."

I knew better than to say another word. So I sat there with my eyes closed, still holding the box of juice. I was thirsty myself, but didn't dare finish it, in case I needed it to soothe Alice.

The door clicked open and Mama stepped from the car. I watched her as she ran through the rain to the covered walkway in front of the motel office. She paused next to the door and lit up a cigarette. The flare of the match gave her face an eerie glow.

"Go in," I whispered. What was she waiting for? I was about to get out of the car when she opened a door and slipped inside the office. It was dimly lit, but I could see her walk up to the front desk.

A light came on inside, turning the office bright. I saw a lady hand Mama a key. She moved close to the window and waved to me, hair rollers bobbing against her head.

I waved back, not wishing to appear unfriendly, or do anything that would make her change her mind and snatch the key from Mama's hand.

"Maybe our luck is changing," Mama said as she threw the car into reverse, drove to the end of the building, and parked in front of room number seven.

"That lady looked real old. Does she live here?"

"I suppose so, seeing as her hair was still in curlers. I told her we've been driving all night, and she was real sweet and said she'd make sure no one disturbed us."

"I'm still tired," I told Mama. "I couldn't sleep all scrunched up in the front seat."

We left most of our stuff in the car. I toted Mabel in her carrier, undid the latch and set her free to explore the room. Mama carried Alice inside and sat her on the toilet, where she peed without waking up.

She put Alice to bed in her clothes, plucking her shoes from her feet before she covered her with the bedspread. I climbed into the other bed, flinging my arms and legs as far as they would stretch, thankful for a real bed.

"The worst is over," said Mama as she kissed me. "We can stay in bed all day." I watched as she double-bolted the door.

"Aren't you coming to bed?" She needed to sleep. Every time I'd woken up the night before, I'd caught Mama awake, staring out the window.

"I need a soak in the bath. I won't be long." She pulled a nightshirt from her overnight bag and disappeared into the bathroom. I fell asleep listening to the rush of water filling the tub.

I awoke several hours later, groggy and confused. I crept over to the window and peered around the side of the drapes. It was black outside, a real dark that told me it was night and we had slept the day away.

Mama called up a local pizza parlor and ordered a pizza with extra cheese. We ate it in bed.

I took a shower and washed my hair. Mama tried to get Alice to take a bath, but she pitched a fit and got to stay in the same smelly clothes she'd been wearing for two days.

At midnight, we turned off the TV and swept the crumbs off the sheets. I helped Mama organize the rest of the stuff she'd brought in from the car.

"This is temporary," she said when she caught me staring at the boxes and bags heaped in the corner.

"Temporary." I repeated the word to myself, the way some people count sheep, to lull myself to sleep.

Hello, God, thank you for the place to stay. I don't want to appear ungrateful, because the Sweetwater Motel is definitely better than sleeping in the car, but to tell you the truth, it's real old and reminds me of motels you see in creepy movies. We are smack-dab in the middle of Ohio. It's called the Buckeye State, but I have yet to see a buckeye, whatever they are. It's real flat here and makes me miss the hills back home.

CHAPTER 6

Alice Lets the Cat Out of the Bag

THE NEXT morning I woke early. I'd tossed and turned most of the night. Mama and Alice lay asleep in their bed. I slipped on my clothes from the day before and looked for something to eat.

There was nothing left but half a piece of cold pizza. I was starving. Sifting through the bottom of Mama's satchel, I found some change, enough for a cold drink. If I played my cards right, I could be back before she woke.

The door locked behind me. I'd forgotten to take the key, but I'd worry about that later. At the moment all I could think about was my empty stomach. Some pancakes sure would taste good.

I located the ice machine in an alcove. A note taped to the wall said COLD DRINKS IN OFFICE. A man and woman staying at the motel sat in the front office at a card table, drinking coffee and reading the morning paper.

"Help yourself, dear." I recognized the lady who'd given Mama the room key. Her red curly hair was piled on her head and anchored with two things that looked like chopsticks from a Chinese restaurant. She wore a purple jumpsuit with metallic gold sneakers and took small, bouncy steps.

She arranged powdered doughnuts into a pyramid. Next to the doughnuts sat pitchers of milk and orange juice, a pot of coffee, and those little boxes of cereal Mama never buys because she says they're too expensive. I recounted the coins in my pocket.

"Oh, you don't need any money. The breakfast comes with the room."

"Thank you. I'd like a doughnut."

"What's your name?" She asked this in a kind way, as if she wanted to be my friend.

I couldn't remember if Mama had said we could use our real names. "Sarah Jane, ma'am. Sarah Jane Otis."

"Well, Sarah Jane, I'm happy to make your acquaintance. My name is Muriel. Muriel Sweetwater. And you may have a doughnut. Have two doughnuts, no one's keeping count."

The couple at the card table left, and Mrs. Sweetwater set a place for me. I'd planned to go back to our room, but I didn't want to hurt her feelings.

"Thank you," I said and sat down to eat.

"You're very welcome. You must be an early riser. Is your mother still sleeping?"

"Yes. My sister is too."

Mrs. Sweetwater sat next to me with her coffee and two doughnuts. She wore three rings on each hand, each set with different colored stones. Very sparkly. "I didn't know there were three of you."

"We can pay you if it costs extra."

She laughed and wiped the sugar from her mouth. "Oh, no, children always stay free. I just meant I didn't see her yesterday morning."

"She fell asleep in the car. Alice is only four years old. I'm twelve."

"Twelve is a wonderful age. But then, every year is a wonderful age if it's what you are. I'll be seventy-two on my next birthday."

I wondered if she expected me to tell her she looked younger. Mama told me no woman ever wanted to look her age, that's why makeup was invented.

Muriel Sweetwater's penciled-in eyebrows arched high above her blue eyes. Half-moons of purple eye shadow matched her outfit.

She settled her cup in its saucer, sat back in her chair, and let out a sigh. "So, are you on vacation?"

"Sort of."

"Did you notice the zoo?"

"Yes, I saw it."

"I have passes, you know," Mrs. Sweetwater said. She got up and disappeared behind the counter. I heard her rummaging through some drawers.

I stuffed the last of the powdered doughnut into my mouth and washed it down with a glass of milk. At the exact moment I was thinking Mama would say we had no time for side trips, she came charging through the door, fierce as a wild animal, Alice tucked under one arm.

"Put me down!" screamed Alice, flailing her skinny legs. Mama practically dropped her on her head.

"Sarah Jane, what do you think you're doing, scaring me to death? I thought you'd been kid-napped or worse." Mama stood there in her nightshirt, barefoot and wild-haired.

"Here they are," said Mrs. Sweetwater, pop-ping up from behind the counter, a bunch of tickets in her hand. "Free passes to the zoo."

Mama stopped dead in her tracks at the sight of Mrs. Sweetwater springing from behind the counter like a jack-in-the-box. If Mama weren't my own flesh and blood, I would not have recog-nized her. Where was the woman who never left the house without a freshly ironed outfit and makeup like a cover girl?

Seeing me safe and sound, she came out of her frenzy and cast an eye on herself, throwing her arms across her chest as if she were naked, instead of covered from her neck to her knees with an Atlanta Braves nightshirt.

"I'm so sorry," she said to Mrs. Sweetwater. "I hope Sarah Jane hasn't been making a pest of herself."

Alice took advantage of the diversion, sashayed over to the breakfast table, and attacked the doughnuts. I poured her a glass of milk so she wouldn't try to do it herself and make a mess. She didn't even say thank you, just stuck her tongue out at me and said, "You're in trouble," with a mouthful of chewed doughnut.

"Am not." I pushed the platter of doughnuts out of her reach.

She kicked me good and hard, but I pretended it didn't hurt.

"Let's go, Sarah Jane," Mama tossed her head like a bossy mare and headed for the door.

"Wouldn't you like some coffee, dear?" asked Mrs. Sweetwater. "It's still nice and hot."

"I'd better get dressed first." Mama pulled at her nightshirt.

"Oh, there's nobody here but us girls. Sit down and have a bite to eat. You look plumb tuckered out."

Mrs. Sweetwater filled a cup with coffee, wrapped a cherry sweet roll in a napkin, and placed them on the card table.

Mama sipped her coffee and smoothed down her wild hair. "I must look a sight."

"Did you come a long way, Mrs. Otis?" Mrs. Sweetwater asked. I wondered what Mama would say.

"Please, call me Becky. And this is Alice, and you've already met Sarah Jane."

I could tell Mama was playing for time, trying to come up with a good answer. "Oh, you know, we're kind of taking a little holiday, seeing the sights." Alice scrambled up on Mama's lap and rested her head on her chest.

"Bless her heart, she's still tired." Mrs. Sweetwater pulled the passes to the zoo from her pocket and held them in front of Alice. "Would you like to see all the beautiful animals?"

Alice lifted her chin and looked at Mama. "Can we, Mama? Please, can we go to the zoo?"

I expected to hear excuses. But Mama surprised me, took the passes from Mrs. Sweetwater's hand and said, "Thanks."

While she ate her breakfast, I noticed a sign with the word LIBRARY in big letters tacked to the wall in the corner. Beneath the sign sat two comfy-looking stuffed chairs, their slipcovers printed with faded palm trees. A hassock sat between the chairs, a place to put your feet up while you read one of the books that lined the shelves.

There hadn't been enough room in our car to bring all my books from home. I had managed to squeeze a few of my favorites under the front passenger seat and sandwich several more between sheets and towels that Mama'd brought along. The rest of my beautiful books, as well as my entire collection of comic books, waited for me at home.

I picked up a Nancy Drew mystery from the bottom shelf of the Sweetwater Motel library. *The Secret of the Hidden Staircase.*

"Take as many as you want," said Mrs. Sweetwater. "That's what they're there for."

I signed out the book on a pad of paper, then sat down next to Mama, out of Alice's kicking range.

"Did you notice the Water Park?" asked Mrs.

Sweetwater. "It's right next door to the zoo. I'll get you some passes for that. My grandkids used to practically live there when they'd visit."

Mama stood up quickly and Alice slipped from her lap. "We won't be staying that long. But thank you anyway. Come on girls, we need to get cleaned up."

"You're very welcome. And Sarah Jane, come back and visit anytime."

Jealousy twisted Alice's face. She didn't like it when I got more attention than she did. "We've got a cat," Alice announced real loud. "Her name is Mabel."

"Now, isn't that lovely," said Mrs. Sweetwater. "You must miss her."

Before Mama could get Alice out the door so she couldn't open her big fat mouth again, she blurted, "I don't miss her. She's in our room. Sleeping in her little house."

Mama pushed Alice behind her and smiled at Mrs. Sweetwater. "I hope you don't mind. She's a good cat and I'll keep her in her crate so she doesn't get any hair in the room."

Alice peered around Mama's side. "Mabel's

very neat. My Grandma Emma's cat pees on the floor and poops in the plants when he gets angry, but Mabel never misses the litter box."

Mrs. Sweetwater leaned down to Alice. "She sounds like a remarkable cat. Tell her I hope she has a nice stay at the Sweetwater Motel." This made Alice laugh, and she ducked behind Mama.

"Thank you so much for understanding." Mama motioned for me to come quick.

"And don't worry about cat hair. I've got a super-duper vacuum that will clean up anything, so let Mabel run around the room."

Mrs. Sweetwater winked at me, and I winked back to be polite. I ran to catch up with Mama and Alice.

Alice insisted on unlocking the door to our room. She skipped to the bathroom and set Mabel free. "Run, Mabel, get your exercise," she yelled as she chased her. Mabel ran under one of the beds to hide from Alice.

Mama grabbed me by the arm and sat me down on the edge of the bed. Her lip quivered, her eyes darkened. "Do not ever pull another stunt like that. Do you hear me, Sarah Jane?"

"Yes, ma'am."

"Do you have any idea what could have happened to you?" I kept quiet, knowing she did not expect an answer, and braced myself for a list of all the evils that lay in wait outside our room, including my daddy, who might be moving closer to us. Instead of harsh words, she let out a sigh, and reached past me for her cigarettes and matches.

"Fix a bath for Alice and sit with her while she washes." She let herself out the door and sat in a chair outside our window, smoking a cigarette and staring at the parking lot and the street beyond.

I poured a little bottle of shampoo under the water faucet to make bubbles. It was the only way I could get Alice into the tub.

"Sarah Jane," said Alice as I filled the ice bucket with warm water and used it to rinse her hair. "When are we going home?"

I didn't know the answer to her question so I did what Mama would do, and changed the subject. "Close your mouth before you get soap in it," I said to her. "And if you want to go to the zoo, you'd better let me help you get dressed real fast before Mama changes her mind."

Alice didn't ask me again about going home. Maybe she forgot about it in her excitement at going to the zoo. Or maybe she didn't want to hear the answer.

"Come on, Alice," I said to her, once she was dried and dressed. "Let's play beauty shop." I sat her on the dresser and fixed her hair the way she liked it. I even let her wear my sparkly butterfly barrettes, the ones I bought with my allowance.

Alice checked herself out in the mirror and then ran outside to Mama. "Ta-da!" she said, twirling in a circle so Mama could properly admire her.

"Are you Miss America?" asked Mama. "I declare, you will outshine the peacocks at the zoo."

Mama came inside to take her shower. As she passed me on her way to the bathroom, she gave me a hug. She didn't say anything, but sometimes a hug is enough.

Okay, God, we are going to the zoo. Mama says we deserve a break. We've been gone for three days. I wonder if Daddy has gone nuts, punching holes in the walls of our house until they resemble Swiss cheese. Or maybe he doesn't care, and he's glad to be rid of us.

CHAPTER 7

The Columbus Zoo

MAMA INSISTED we clean out the car and run a few errands before we could go to the zoo.

"What's your hurry, Sarah Jane? The place doesn't open for another hour."

I noticed she spent time doing her makeup and she dressed in a nice pair of white slacks and a sleeveless black shirt. Her painted pink toenails peeked out from her white leather sandals, sparkly as small jewels.

After we picked up a few things at the market, we parked in front of a place called MJ Realty.

A fierce moist heat rose from the sidewalk, causing Alice's soft blond hair to curl around her face. My own brown hair hung limp to my shoulders; I pulled it back and fastened it with a rubber band I found in the pocket of my shorts. I was admiring color photos of houses displayed on the window of MJ Realty, imagining what it would be like to live in the red brick house with the white roses, when Mama brought me back to my senses.

"Don't waste your time looking at those." Mama nudged Alice toward the door.

"Then why are we here?"

"They list rentals too. That's what we're looking for, a nice apartment near some good schools."

The real estate office, its air as cool as ice water, stood quiet. Mama sat Alice on a bench.

"Keep her busy while I talk to somebody."

A lady sat behind a desk working at a computer. "May I help you?" The calendar on the wall, turned to the month of August, reminded me school would start soon.

"Yes, ma'am," said Mama. "We're looking to rent a place nearby. That is, if the schools are good."

"They're excellent," said the lady, sitting up extra straight, as if that would make the schools seem even better.

"Those are my girls, so it's important that the schools are good." Mama pointed to us, and I smiled. Alice picked at a loose thread on the seat cushion.

I gave Alice some pamphlets to keep her busy.

"House or apartment?" The lady asked Mama.

"I beg your pardon?" said Mama.

"Are you interested in renting a house or an apartment?"

I wanted to say real loud, "A *house*, we want a house," because I'd never lived in an apartment. It was important to get a place like the one we had left, so we wouldn't wake up each day and wonder where we were.

The receptionist told Mama there was no one in the office who could help her right then, but she could make an appointment for later that morning.

"The zoo," I whispered to Mama.

"What about later this afternoon? My girls and I are going to the zoo today."

The receptionist checked something on her computer. "How does five o'clock work for you?"

"Perfect," said Mama.

When we got in the car, I took one of the pamphlets filled with glossy color photos of houses to browse through.

"It says this one has three bathrooms and two fireplaces." I ran my finger over a picture of a brick house.

Mama glanced at the rose-colored house. "Take a gander at the price, baby girl. It's $450,000. That's almost half a million dollars."

"Maybe it's for rent." I would be happy sleeping in the basement of that house.

"Even if it is for rent, we couldn't afford it." She slipped a booklet that said *Apartment Guide* on the cover into her purse. "Most of those houses are for sale. We can't afford to buy a house right now."

"But we will one day, won't we?"

She reached out and patted my hand. "Sure we will. Just as soon as I get a job and save some money. You'll see, things will work out."

Back home, Mama would always tell me

things would work out. Maybe she said it to make me feel better. I doubted she believed it anymore.

We must have been the first customers at the zoo. We drove up to the ticket booth, no waiting in line. Mama showed our passes to a skinny boy wearing a COLUMBUS ZOO T-shirt and he waved us through to the parking lot.

Alice spied the gift shop first thing. Mama had to drag her away, promising to buy her something before we left. Alice probably would have been happy spending the day indoors with the fake animals.

"All right, baby girls, let's have us an adventure." Mama tightened her grip on Alice and winked at me.

I knew it must be hard for her to pretend things were normal, so I made a promise to myself to do my best to go along with whatever she did.

After we'd seen enough animals and ate lunch, we strolled through an area shaded by tall trees that opened onto the river.

Mama counted money from her pocket. "Who wants to go for a boat ride?" she asked.

"It's the Scioto," the ticket taker said when Mama asked him the name of the river. "It meets up with the Olentangy River in Columbus."

We found a place near the back, apart from the rest of the tourists who crowded into the front seats. Alice sat on Mama's lap so she could look for fish in the water.

Mama smiled at me. "Some day I'm going to take a real cruise. Like the ones you see in the movies where everybody gets dressed up fancy for dinner and there's music and dancing every night. You'll see, Sarah Jane, you'll see. Our luck will change."

The boat pulled away from the dock, cutting through water murky as pea soup, too dark to see any fish. A breeze came off the river, cooling my skin.

Looking over to the riverbank on the opposite shore, I tried to pick out where the Sweetwater Motel sat hidden behind dark pines. When we got back to the motel, I'd see if I could walk though those pines to get to the water. It couldn't hurt to have an escape route, just in case.

I hope you're not busy, God, but this won't take long. I'm beginning to worry that running away from home was the biggest mistake of our lives. I know Daddy was mean, but why couldn't Mama have figured out a way for us to stay in our own house? She's going to look at apartments. If we can't go home, can you at least help her find a real nice one with a big bedroom for me and maybe my own bathroom, because Alice forgets to flush the toilet, and it's disgusting? That's all for now. Oh, I almost forgot, this is Sarah Jane Otis, still stuck in room number seven of the Sweetwater Motel.

CHAPTER 8

Mama Disappears

ALICE FELL ASLEEP on the boat. Mama managed to get her past the gift shop, into the car, and back to the motel before she woke up.

"Get Sister out of the car," Mama said, already fidgeting in her bag for a cigarette.

Alice opened her eyes and blinked a few times. Her lip began to quiver when she realized she'd been tricked.

"No, no!" she screamed, punching at me when I tried to unfasten the belt holding her booster seat in place. "I want to go to the gift shop. You promised."

"I didn't promise you anything, so stop hitting me." I pushed her hands away.

Mama turned and fixed me with her eyes. "Oh, for goodness' sake. Don't stand there arguing with her. Get her out of the car before she heats up."

When I tried again to get close enough to undo her seat belt, she tried to bite me. I jumped back and whacked my head on the car.

"You do it, Mama. She's being a brat." I backed away rubbing my head.

Mama threw down her cigarette, squishing it with the ball of her foot.

"Alice, I will not put up with your nonsense today."

Mama needed help. If Alice put her in a bad mood, she might not get a good apartment.

"Hey, Alice, they've got a pool here. We can go swimming." She stopped kicking the back of the seat.

"There now, doesn't that sound nice? If you're a good girl for Mama, I'll take you swimming as soon as I get back from my appointment with the apartment lady."

Alice let Mama help her from the car. "I want to swim now." She spun on her heels and jammed her hands on her hips.

"Not now, Alice." Mama looked at her watch. "I have just enough time to clean up and get over to that office by five."

"If she wears her swimmies, I could watch her while you're gone." I could have used a swim myself. It must have been a hundred degrees.

Mama hesitated for a minute. "No, you two'd better come with me."

She took hold of Alice by the hand and pulled her toward our room. Alice refused to budge; she slumped to the ground, dead weight. I thought her arm would pop out of its socket.

"I want to swim!" she screamed. "Swim, swim, swim!"

A dark look, with the warning of a storm cloud, crossed Mama's face. She wasted no time on sweet talk, but picked up Alice and carried her football style under her arm. Alice flailed her arms and kicked her legs so fast, she looked as if she were swimming through air. I ran ahead of them, took the room key from Mama's hand, and unlocked the door.

Mama deposited Alice in the chair by the window, slammed the door shut, and bolted it twice. I could tell she was trying real hard to stay calm, because she closed her eyes and took ten deep breaths.

"Find something on television for her. I have to get ready." Mama glanced at herself in the mirror over the dresser. "The way I look, those people wouldn't rent me a doghouse."

I found a cartoon show for Alice and settled her on the bed. With two pillows behind her head and her blankie on her chest, Alice took two sniffs of that rag and fell asleep.

"It's the heat," said Mama as she came into the room, her hair slicked into a ponytail, her peach lipstick glossy as satin. "Alice never could stand the heat. It seems a shame to wake her."

"I'll stay with her." I wanted to go and see the apartments, to make sure Mama got the nicest one, but I knew she could get more done without Alice tagging along.

"Promise you won't open the door to anyone.

And no peeking out the drapes. Someone could see you."

"No one will know we're in here."

She leaned over and kissed me on my nose. "I'll be back before you know it."

The door closed behind her, and I wondered if it would be okay to take a nap myself. Two minutes later Mama returned with two frosted cans of Coca-Cola and a package of peanut-butter crackers.

"Alice can have hers when she wakes up." She paused at the door, pointing to the dead bolt. "Turn this after I leave and don't open it until you hear my voice. Maybe we should have a secret code."

"Scioto," I said. "Like the river. Say Scioto through the door and I'll know it's you and not somebody pretending."

Mama tapped her forehead, as if she were locking the word inside. "Scioto it is."

I deposited Mabel in the bathroom. "Here, now eat this and stay out of trouble." I poured a handful of kibble into her bowl and shut the door so she couldn't come back into the bedroom

and wake Alice by climbing on the bed and
meowing.

I finished off my drink in six swallows, but
left the crackers for Alice. She liked to be the one
to open the cellophane package, to hear the crin-
kling sound.

It made me sleepy to see her lying there
so peacefully. With the draperies pulled tight and
only the flickering light of the TV, it could have
been ten o'clock at night instead of five in the
afternoon.

I fell into a sound sleep. Images of big
houses filled my dreams, their floors covered in
carpet so thick you could sink up to your ankles.
In my dream, Mama stood at the sink in a
yellow kitchen, the worry lines erased from her
face.

I woke with a start, an uneasy feeling causing
me to sit up and check the time. It was after eight
o'clock. Where could Mama be? How long could
it take to see a few apartments?

No one knew where we were, except Mama.
What if she'd been in a car wreck? *Please let
Mama be safe*, I prayed, cutting it short so I could

concentrate on making a list of who to call if she never returned.

How could she leave us like that, all alone in a stupid motel with nothing to eat but peanut-butter crackers? What was I supposed to tell Alice when she woke up asking for Mama?

I thought of Mrs. Sweetwater and how nice she'd been to us, giving us doughnuts and free passes to the zoo. But if I told her the truth, she might call the police and tell them we were abandoned, left alone in room number seven.

Daddy would come and get us, but he'd be angry. And maybe he'd want only Alice, and he'd leave me in an orphanage or one of those homes for runaway kids because I had taken sides with Mama.

The only person I could trust was Grandma Emma, Mama's own mother. She'd know what to do. I picked up the phone, my hand shaking, and dialed her number. It rang once, twice. I heard a rap on the door. I hung up the phone. Pressing my ear to the door, I heard a voice saying *"Scioto"* through the wood panel. *"Scioto, Scioto,"* over and over again.

"Sarah Jane, it's me, Mama. Open the door!"

I turned the bolt and slid off the chain. "It's about time."

Mama pushed past me carrying a pizza and a take-out bag from Wendy's. She dumped everything on the dresser. "Clear off that table so we can eat."

I piled up the brochures and Alice's My Little Pony collection from the round table by the window and dumped everything on the floor. Alice remained as sound asleep as a bear in winter. Soft whistles escaped her nose.

How could Mama walk in there barking orders at me like nothing had happened? I ran to the bathroom, climbed into the tub, pulled the shower curtain closed and crouched into a ball, my back against the cool porcelain.

Alice must have woken, because I heard her give out a whimper and then change her tune when Mama told her there was pizza with extra cheese, and chocolate shakes.

"Come and eat before it gets cold." Mama's voice got closer. I saw her shape through the shower curtain. "What are you doing in there?"

I didn't answer, couldn't speak if I wanted to, my words jammed inside me.

Mama sat on the edge of the tub. "Did something happen while I was gone?"

"Can I have Sarah Jane's shake?" Alice yelled from the bedroom. Mama ignored her and peeked around the side of the curtain.

I didn't realize I was crying until she reached over with her hand and began to wipe away my tears. "Let's get you out of here," she said, gripping under my arms and trying to pull me up.

When she couldn't move me, she climbed into the tub, tipping me forward so she could wedge herself behind me. She hugged me to her and rocked me the way she used to when we sat in the chair back home, reading stories.

"Tell me, baby girl. Tell me what's wrong."

"I thought you were dead." I stared at the faucet at the other end of the tub. One drop of water hung suspended, ready to fall.

"Now, why would you think a thing like that?"

"Because you were gone for hours, Mama, you could have been to the moon and back."

"I'm sorry, but that woman dragged me in and out of more apartments than I could count. I had no idea how late it was."

I shoved off her legs and moved to the other end of the tub. The faucet pressed into my back, the dripping water soaked into my shirt. "You could have called. We do have a phone, you know."

"You're right, but I was afraid if I woke Alice, you'd have a time keeping her out of the pool."

"Yeah, well, you should have called. Don't ever do that again."

"I promise. Now will you forgive me?"

Before we left home, on an ordinary day, I would have stretched out my forgiveness, made her wait a day or two before I acted as if everything was okay. But that night I realized more than ever how small my family had become and how much I needed to feel close to her.

I stood and got out of the tub. "I suppose."

"Good. Now let's eat. I'm starving."

Alice had taken advantage of being left to her own devices, finishing her shake and half of mine, the front of her shirt covered with choco-late dribbles. She'd eaten the cheese off two pieces of pizza and was reaching for a third when Mama slapped her hand and told her to get into her bathing suit if she wanted to go swimming before the pool closed.

I didn't have much of an appetite, but I ate one piece of pizza to please Mama. We squeezed Alice into her swimmies, gathered a few towels, and walked to the pool.

We had the place to ourselves. Mama reclined in a lounge chair, smoking a cigarette and sipping a wine cooler she'd fetched from the car. "Just this one little drink," she said when she saw the look on my face.

I stayed in the shallow end with Alice, pulling her through the water, pretending to be a tugboat.

"Make the noise," she said, and I'd say "Toot, toot," until she laughed.

Mama finished her drink and sat at the edge of the pool near Alice so I could jump off the wall at the deep end. I liked to open my eyes underwater and swim up to the lights. I wished I could breathe underwater. It was so peaceful and far away from what was waiting for me on the surface, my real life.

"Time for bed," Mama said, her voice a murmur. From where I sat at the bottom of the pool, I could see her leaning over the water, her ponytail swinging around the side of her face, everything about her soft and wavy, like in a dream.

I burst from the water and the cool night air turned my skin to goose flesh. Mama wrapped me in a towel, gathered up our things, and hustled us back to our room. I noticed the red truck parked in the same place and a station wagon with New York license plates. No sign of Daddy's Buick.

It didn't occur to me until I was about to drop off to sleep that I'd forgotten to ask Mama about our new apartment.

"Mama," I whispered. "Did you find us a nice place?"

"Hush, now. I'll tell you all about it in the morning."

"School's starting soon and you have to sign me up."

"Don't you think I know that?" I heard her rustle the covers.

"I just meant that we have to know where we're going to be living so we can give the school people our address."

"I have it handled, so stop your worrying."

"I don't have to have my own room, but it would be nice."

Mama reached across the space between our two beds and squeezed my hand. "I would buy you a castle if I could, you know that, don't you?"

"Yes, ma'am."

"Then you have to trust that everything will be okay. Can you do that for me?"

"Yes. I can do that."

"And will you do one more thing for me?"

"What's that?"

"Please, go to sleep."

"Night-night, Mama."

"Sweet dreams, baby girl."

Thank you for bringing Mama back to us last night. I've never been that scared in my life. Not even that night we had to run through the storm to Grandma Emma's. Even when Mama's with us, it worries me to think we have only one parent. At least with two parents you have a spare in case something happens to one of them. The good news is Mama found us an apartment so we won't be at the Sweetwater Motel much longer. I'm sad we won't have our own house, but at least this new place won't have holes in the walls.

CHAPTER 9

The Bridal Suite

MAMA TRIED TO make up for the night before. She woke Alice and me at seven and told us if we got dressed real quick, she'd treat us to breakfast.

"See here," she said as she pointed to a restaurant advertised in the phone book. "This looks like a good one. They serve pancakes, waffles, you name it, they've got it."

It wasn't easy getting clean clothes on Alice, since she refused to put down her tattered blankie. I wrenched the rag from one hand and put it in the other so I could wrangle her into a T-shirt. The hair fairies must have come during the night and spun her fine hair into blond webs.

She screamed when I tried to untangle them with a plastic comb.

"Forget it," said Mama. She leaned into the dresser mirror and applied black mascara to her lashes. Her own hair looked like a model's, held back with a red headband and brushed till it gleamed. She wore a red tank top and short-shorts that showed off her tanned legs. Daddy didn't like her to wear that outfit out of the house.

I gave up on Alice's hair and rummaged through my suitcase for something nice to wear. It didn't make sense to put away my clothes in the dresser if we were going to move to our new place in a day or two.

"Is this too wrinkled?" I asked Mama. She inspected me in my white jumper with a blue-and-white-checked shirt. With my red boots, of course.

"You look fine. Let's get this show on the road."

Mama strapped in Alice, cranked open all the windows, and then took me aside. She lit up a cigarette, and from the way her hands shook, I knew better than to remind her that smoking was hazardous to her health. "There's been a change of plans."

Happy anticipation filled my heart, that feeling you get when you're holding a beautifully wrapped gift and you're sure it's just what you asked for fifty million times. Maybe us leaving home was what Daddy needed to shake him up and to make him change.

I waited for Mama to tell me she'd talked to him and that we could go home and be a family again. A happy family.

She gave Alice a stick of gum to keep her busy, then drew me over to a pair of chairs under a tree. "You remember how I was gone so long last night?"

"Yes. Three hours and forty-five minutes." Maybe she'd stopped at a pay phone and called home collect. And Daddy told her how much he missed us.

"Well, I saw more apartments than I ever want to see again in my life. That woman, her name was Betty, was nice and all, but she and I weren't on the same wavelength."

"What do you mean?"

"The first apartment she showed me cost over a thousand dollars a month. So I said to her, 'Betty, I can't afford this much,' and she says, 'Well, if you want to stay in this town, that's what it's going to cost.'"

"So, did you go to another town?"

"Not at first. Betty looked at her listings book and came up with a couple that were cheaper, but not by much. Finally—it must have been past dinnertime and I could tell Betty wanted to get home in the worst way—she shows me one about ten miles from here. It wasn't bad and the price was okay."

"So, did you get it? How many bathrooms does it have?"

Mama offered me a piece of gum. "I was all ready to sign on the dotted line, when I read the fine print. Sarah Jane, there is no way we can afford our own place right now. We'd have to come up with two months' rent, deposits for all the utilities—that's the phone and stuff—and on top of that we'd still have to buy furniture. It would take every cent I have to get us a place, and then we'd have to sleep on the floor and eat off paper plates."

Okay, I thought, now she's going to tell me she realized we'd made a mistake and that's when she called Daddy and they made up and we were going home as soon as we ate breakfast and packed up the car.

"Mama," screamed Alice from the car.

"Coming, baby girl." Mama took hold of my hand, her eyes locked with mine. "Things will work out, you'll see. I just need a few days to figure something out. And I have to find a job. That's what I need. A good job so I can make some money."

"How long will it take to get enough money?"

"I have no idea."

"Longer than a week?"

"More like six months."

"We can't live in a motel for that long."

"Mrs. Sweetwater told me she'd give us a good deal if we helped with the chores and took care of the place when she takes a day off."

"I want to go home."

Mama put out her cigarette. "Well, we can't, so let's not even talk about it."

Alice let out another fierce scream. Mama

walked to the car, me lagging behind. We got in and headed for town. I gazed from my window at the beautiful homes that lined the streets, their lawns lush as green carpets. A girl rode a shiny bike on her driveway; a little dog ran beside her.

Maybe I had some of my daddy's meanness inside me, because I wanted her to crash her bike. I hated her for being able to ride on her own driveway, and for getting to live in a beautiful house.

Mama and Alice sang along to the radio, but I stayed mute, too sad to utter a sound. At that moment, any hope I had deserted me and floated out the open window to find its way to that girl. We would never fit in, in Dublin or any other town. We were homeless.

Alice stuffed herself with pancakes soaked in syrup. Mama ate a cheese omelet and drank the better part of a pot of coffee, but I could barely finish my cereal. All I could think about was my room back home. I wondered if it missed me, and knew I was gone and never coming back.

Mama paid the bill and gave each of us a

candy mint from a bowl near the cash register. We listened to the radio on the way back to the motel, passing along Muirfield Drive. The road cut through a place called Muirfield Village, very fancy by the looks of a swimming pool and pond surrounded by beautiful flower beds. Alice wanted to stop at the pond and feed the ducks, but Mama said it was private property.

The Sweetwater Motel parking lot stood empty. Even the red truck was gone from in front of room number one. Mama handed me the key to our room and told me to check on Mabel and get Alice to brush her teeth.

"Where are you going?"

"I'm going to have a little talk with Mrs. Sweetwater about our accommodations."

Alice brushed her teeth without a protest when I promised she could watch TV if she did a good job. Even with all the lights on, it felt like we were living in a cave. I opened the drapes to let in some daylight. If Daddy came and saw our car, closed draperies would not stop him from getting to us.

A few minutes later Mama knocked at the

door. I opened it and she motioned for me to come outside. "Bring the key," she said. "In case Sister gets it in her head to lock us out."

Alice lay on her stomach on the floor in a trance, watching the shopping network.

Mama passed me a cold drink, a peace offering if I ever saw one. I had a hunch she had more bad news to share with me—why else would she take me where Alice couldn't overhear?

She perched on the edge of one of the turquoise metal chairs in front of our room. I took the other one; a pot of geraniums sat between us like a referee.

"Okay, now." Mama sat up straight and pulled her headband from her hair, playing with the ends. "You remember how Mrs. Sweetwater said she has special rates?" She didn't wait for an answer. "Well, we can stay here month to month until we get our act together."

A groan seeped from my lips. School would be starting soon. What would she write in the place marked HOME ADDRESS when she registered me? And where would the bus pick me up?

"Sarah Jane, are you listening to me?"

I stared at Mama, but the words would not come.

She nudged me with her toe. "Don't go getting all hot under the collar before you hear me out. We can stay here real cheap, for practically nothing if we help out a bit with the chores. I can still get a job and I'll be able to save most of my salary toward getting us a nice apartment. It just makes sense to take advantage of her hospitality, now doesn't it?"

At that moment, nothing made sense. I pictured Alice and me dressed in shiny pink uniforms, with babushkas on our heads, scrubbing mold from the bathroom tiles and scouring the toilets.

I was about to ask Mama if she'd lost her mind when Mrs. Sweetwater came toward us, doing that bouncy walk, smiling like she'd won the lottery. She wore a turquoise-blue pants suit, the color of the chairs we sat on, matching sneakers, and white flower earrings the size of saucers.

"Here's the key," she said and peeked into our room where Alice was pretending to talk on the phone to Mary Beth, her favorite home-shopping hostess. "Do you want the little one to come with us?"

"Alice, come with Mama. That show will be on when you get back."

"I was going to buy you a necklace," said Alice. She liked to pretend she had enough money to order anything she wanted. Sometimes she made me keep a tally of her pretend purchases.

"That's real nice of you, but right now Mrs. Sweetwater is going to show us another room."

We walked to the end of the building where it turned a corner and made an L shape. "This is the bridal suite," announced Mrs. Sweetwater. She laughed when she said this. "These rooms were originally an apartment for my parents. When Mr. Sweetwater and I built this place, we wanted to turn it into a bridal suite."

Mrs. Sweetwater turned the key in the lock and opened the door wide. Mama motioned for me to step into what had to be the living room. A couch covered in palm-tree fabric, similar to the chairs in the motel office, sat against the far wall.

Two of the ugliest lamps I'd ever seen, giant blowfish with crinkly shades, took up most of the tops of mismatched end tables.

"The couch opens up into a bed," said Mrs. Sweetwater.

"Oh, this is nice, isn't it, girls?" Mama touched one of the lampshades, trimmed with pretend seashells.

"I like it," said Alice. "It's big, so I can twirl." She twirled herself right into a fake plant, tipping it on its side. Dust from the leaves floated through the air.

The air smelled stale, like an attic filled with old clothes. I wrinkled my nose at Mama, and she gave me a warning look. Mrs. Sweetwater led us down a hallway. A door opened to a bathroom on one side and to a bedroom on the other. The two double beds had faded orange bedspreads. Both of the bedspreads had cigarette burns that resembled bullet holes.

"You girls can have the bedroom and I'll sleep on the sofa bed," said Mama.

Mrs. Sweetwater clapped her hands together and smiled like that lady who sold jewelry on TV.

"Won't that be lovely? You girls will have your own place."

I bit my tongue to keep from saying, *Whoop-dee-doo, our very own bedroom with matching bullet hole bedspreads.*

Alice mimicked Mrs. Sweetwater and clapped her hands.

"Over here's the kitchenette." Mrs. Sweetwater continued with the tour.

"What's a kitchenette?" Alice pulled on Mrs. Sweetwater's sleeve.

"A very small kitchen, like in Barbie's playhouse."

Mama frowned at me. I noticed a door leading outdoors, walked over, and turned the knob. A rusted chair sat abandoned on the grass, its webbed seat sagged.

Mrs. Sweetwater opened the refrigerator. "Everything's in working order, even the ice maker. I had Henry check all the appliances."

Alice peeked inside. "Who's Henry?"

"Henry Buckner. He refers to himself as the Sweetwater Motel handyman, but I call him a miracle worker. The man can fix anything."

The word *miracle* rang in my ears. Mama said it would take a miracle for my daddy to change.

Alice needed details. "Could he fix my doll? Her head's all loosey-goosey."

"I believe he might be able to help you out," said Mrs. Sweetwater.

"Where is Henry?" asked Alice, opening and closing cabinet doors as if she might find him hiding inside.

"Oh, he's usually around someplace. He lives in room number one. If you see his red truck, that means he's home."

So we weren't the only people stuck living at the motel. I wondered what hard luck story this Henry had to tell.

Mama touched my hand, her eyes pleading for help, a kind word, anything to make this easier. "So what do you think, Sarah Jane? Will this do?"

What could I say? If Daddy really cared, he would have found us by now. I felt cheated, as if all the love I'd felt for him and all the forgiveness that was in my heart had been wasted. Wasted on a man who didn't care.

I should have been relieved to get out of room number seven. Our stuff from home sat piled in corners, on chairs, and between the beds. Empty take-out containers littered the dresser top. You had to walk sideways to get from the bed to the bathroom. And even then you were in danger of stepping on one of Alice's tiny toy pieces, which could cause serious injury if you happened to be barefooted. Alice drove me crazy with the TV going day and night. Mama slept through all the noise, getting out of bed just long enough to fetch us something to eat and to sneak a cigarette.

I should have been happy to move from one cramped room into three. But something I saw in the bridal suite caused a ping in my heart. A subtle warning.

It sounds stupid, but I swear it was that refrigerator. A refrigerator big enough to hold a week's worth of groceries. It made our temporary stay at the Sweetwater Motel seem permanent.

Suddenly, the thought of Daddy finding us and dragging us home was less scary than the prospect of spending our days at the Sweetwater

Motel. I'd had enough adventure to last me for the rest of my life. I wanted to go home.

"Well, Sarah Jane, what do you think?" Mama waited for my answer. She had twisted her hair into a corkscrew so tight, I feared she'd be left bald.

"It's fine," I said.

"I like the ice maker," said Alice. "What do you like the best, Sarah Jane?"

I pretended to give my answer some thought. "I like those fish lamps. They're really something."

God, I am so annoyed I could walk all the way back to Georgia, which is what I might do if Mama can't figure out a way to get us an apartment. This morning I had to make the bed in room number four, and I will not even tell you what I found in the sheets, except to say it was disgusting. The other news is that Mama's taking me to register for middle school. I'm nervous they might not let me in because we live in a motel, so please keep working on finding us our own apartment. Thank you and amen.

CHAPTER 10

The Bus Doesn't Stop at the Sweetwater Motel

AFTER WE finished changing sheets, scrubbing bathrooms, and washing the dirty laundry, Mama took me to register for middle school. A nice lady in the front office gave us a tour of the school, starting with the library. Seeing all the books lined up neatly on the shelves made me miss my own books.

Sunshine flooded a courtyard, its pathways paved with bricks engraved with people's names. I wished I had my name engraved in a brick back home, something to say I was there, that I counted.

Alice ran around the gymnasium, shouting her name until it echoed off the walls. I wanted her to hush up, so the office lady wouldn't get the wrong impression and think we didn't have manners. That we were trash.

Mama began to fill out the forms, but she hesitated when she came to the place for our address.

She gave me a tiny smile, and wrote "The Sweetwater Motel" in her back-slanted script.

"Is this okay?" she asked the office lady. "We're staying there until we find an aparment."

The lady furrowed her brow. "Wait here for a minute," she said, and disappeared into a room behind her desk. I heard her talking to someone on the phone.

Mama squeezed my hand. I squeezed back.

The lady returned with a smile on her face. "There now, you are all set." She handed a thick packet to me and told me to read it carefully and if we had any questions to give her a call.

"Thank you." I clutched the envelope to my chest.

"You're very welcome. I checked the bus route, but the bus doesn't stop where you're staying. Would you like me to give them a call and see if they can add it to their route?"

Mama and I both said "No," at the same time.

"Sarah Jane can walk to the nearest stop." Mama stared at me until I nodded in agreement.

"There is one other thing," said the office lady. "If you don't have a permanent address in six weeks, you'll have to pay out-of-district tuition."

"How much is that?" Mama asked.

"I don't have the exact figure, but it's probably at least three thousand dollars for the year."

"Three thousand dollars?" Mama's voice rose high enough to call in the hounds. "Don't you worry, we'll be in our own place long before six weeks."

The office lady almost looked relieved herself. "Welcome to middle school. I hope you have a good year."

"I will," I said, and walked as fast as I could

down the hallway and out of the building before she could change her mind and take back my packet of school papers.

"Man, I am sweating like a pig," said Mama. "For a minute there I was worried she was going to give us a hard time."

"Look at me," yelled Alice. "I'm sweating like a pig too."

"You are not." I helped her into the car and buckled her in.

"Am too. Mama and I are sweating like pigs." She stuck out her tongue to make her point.

"You know, I believe you're right. Your skin is shiny as butter left in the sun."

I didn't feel like arguing with her. Besides, I could afford to be nice to her now that I had a place to go every day. A beautiful school with a library filled with books that I could check out by the bagful, free of charge.

"Maybe you'll make friends with a girl who lives in one of these houses," Mama said as we sped past some of the beautiful homes we saw in the brochures. "Wouldn't that be something?"

"Yes, ma'am, that would be something."

Where do you live? they'd ask me. *I live in a penthouse apartment so high in the sky, clouds float past my window,* I'd say. *I live in a castle with ten fireplaces and a pond filled with fish made of real gold.*

Mama patted my head. "What are you thinking, Sarah Jane?"

"I'm thinking we're going to need a miracle to be able to save enough money for our own place."

"You worry too much. Things will work out."

"You worry too much, Sarah Jane," Alice butted in from the backseat.

What did she know about worrying? She wasn't the one who had to go to school and try to fit in. I'd have bet my red boots that most of those kids lived in fancy houses with parents who didn't try to kill each other.

I envied Alice. The only time she had to pretend was when she played dress-up or paper dolls. I had to pretend all the time. Pretend that everything was okay, pretend to be normal. I would have to leave the real Sarah Jane Otis behind and reinvent myself if I wanted to survive middle school.

As soon as we got back to the motel, I drew forty-two boxes on a piece of paper. Six weeks equaled forty-two days. That's how long we had to get a real place to live.

Someone left a five-dollar tip on the dresser in room number two. Mrs. Sweetwater told me to keep it. I wish I could buy a new pair of jeans and a nice top for school. But I am thankful I have my red boots. They fit just fine.

CHAPTER 11

The Man in Room Number One

AFTER LUNCH, we swam in the motel pool. Mama said we deserved to pamper ourselves, because between helping with the motel chores and whatever job she got, there was no telling the next chance she'd have a minute to relax.

Alice and I played Storm at Sea, making waves and splashing each other and pretending we had to take shelter under one of the lounge chairs until the storm passed. Mama dozed off. I hated to wake her, but Alice was beginning to resemble a canned ham, all sweaty and pink.

I touched Mama gently on the shoulder. She sat up, her eyes wide, as if she was in the middle of a dream.

"Alice doesn't look so good." I stood Alice in front of her.

She pressed a finger against Alice's skin. "Oh, no, she's burned to a crisp. Why did you let me sleep? What's the matter with you, Sarah Jane? You should have put more sunscreen on her."

"Don't blame me. You're the one who fell asleep. You should be happy I didn't let her drown."

"Watch your mouth, missy." She sprang from her chair, grabbing hold of my arms to steady herself. "I am the mama here. So the next time you feel like sassing me, remember I am all you have right now."

I gathered up our things and followed Mama and Alice back to the motel, making ugly faces at her back.

"Be careful not to wake Sister," Mama warned me, after she'd slathered Alice with lotion and put her down for a nap. "I've got to find myself a job lickety-split." She sat at the kitchen table, a newspaper opened to the Help Wanted ads, a fat pink marker in one hand.

By the time Alice woke from her nap, Mama had two job interviews lined up.

"Do you girls think you can stay out of trouble while I'm gone?"

Alice looked up from dunking a cookie into her milk, her concentration broken. "I'll be good. Will you bring me a cherry sucker?"

"I will surely try," said Mama. "Mind Sarah Jane. Stay away from the swimming pool and out of the sun. And no using the stove. I'll get some groceries while I'm out and make us a nice supper."

"What if Alice gets hungry before you get back?"

"Make her peanut-butter crackers. That will hold her. Now, how do I look?" Mama'd changed to a light blue gauzy skirt and white eyelet blouse.

"You look like a princess," I told her.

"Let's go get some cold pop," I suggested to Alice when I got tired of adding up her pretend TV purchases.

We had the motel office to ourselves. Alice insisted on getting her own drink. She liked to deposit the coins and hear the *kerclunk* sound as the can dropped.

I settled in with my drink and a stack of magazines, propping my feet on a hassock in the library corner. I was in no hurry to get back to our rooms.

"I want to go now," Alice said in a high whiny voice that could drill a hole through concrete.

"Don't you want to look at some books?"

She grabbed one about a girl who rode cows.

The door to Mrs. Sweetwater's apartment opened. A tall, skinny man wearing denim overalls and a red T-shirt appeared. His gray hair stood away from his head as if he'd been yanking on it. His oval face looked stretched like a reflection on the back of a spoon.

"Hello, young ladies. I didn't hear you come in. Muriel's kitchen sink is stopped up again."

So this was the handyman Mrs. Sweetwater told us about. The miracle worker.

"I'm Sarah Jane, and this is my sister, Alice. We're staying in the bridal suite."

He nodded his head. "Muriel told me a nice family had moved in there. I'm pleased to meet you." He walked from behind the counter and offered his hand. "I'm Henry Buckner."

"Do you live here?" Alice shook his hand.

"Yes, I do. Been here five years. I have room number one. I guess that makes us neighbors."

"We're not staying long," I said. "This is temporary."

He smiled and nodded again. I think it was his way of saying he understood.

Outside, the sky darkened and thunder boomed in the distance. Alice pressed her face against the window.

"Come away from there," I said, worried the lightning might come through the glass and zap Alice where she stood.

I glanced at Henry. Why would anyone want to live at a motel for five years? I wondered if he was running away from something or someone, like we were.

For now, we were free from my daddy, but I never realized how much our freedom would cost us.

At least at home I had my grandma Emma and my best friend Marion, and I got to live in a real house. And I didn't have to worry about getting kicked out of school because I didn't have a permanent address.

Grandma Emma used to tell me I jumped the gun, and imagined the worst before I took a step back to examine the whole picture. If she was right, I needed to hope for the best, but I couldn't help thinking that running away from Daddy was a big mistake.

Alice sat with Henry at the table by the window, her head bowed in concentration over a little kid's jigsaw puzzle. Henry held a puzzle piece in his fingers, waiting patiently for Alice to make up her mind about where it should go.

"Over here, Henry," she said, dabbing her index finger against an open space. "It's the bunny's ear."

As soon as Henry fit the piece in place, Alice handed him another. He glanced over at me and smiled. "Excuse me, Alice," he said.

He came over to where I sat reading my book, reached above me and switched on the light.

"You're going to ruin your eyes reading in the dark that way."

"I didn't notice," I said.

"That's what my wife always told me when I found her with her eyes about two inches from the page, lost in some book. She liked mysteries too. Used to read five a week." His face softened as he talked about his wife.

"My daddy used to tell me the same thing, that I was ruining my eyes."

"I don't believe I've met your daddy."

"He couldn't come, he had to stay home and work."

"Well, I'm sure he misses you."

"Yes. I miss him too." It seemed the polite thing to say, but as soon as the words left my mouth, I realized I did miss him.

I missed hanging out with him and fixing cars. Daddy and I liked doing the same things, like sitting by the river for hours and fishing. Mama said she'd take me one day, but it's not the same if the other person doesn't like it as much as you. Losing Daddy from my life was like driving a car with only half the spark plugs firing. It didn't feel right.

Henry wandered back to the table to assist Alice. I pretended to read my book, but I didn't see the words. My mind drifted back to the good times. Alice got Mama's beautiful singing voice, but I got Daddy's talent for taking things apart and putting them back together again.

On Saturdays he used to let me help him work on the junkers he kept under tarps behind our house. At first all I could do was hand him the tools, kind of like a nurse in an operating room, but I worked my way up to changing spark plugs and air filters. He said we were a team.

I pictured myself going with Daddy to the auto-parts store, loading everything into his car, and restocking the shelves at the service station. Afterward, we'd prop our feet on his desk, share a pizza, and talk about how we were going to decorate the place for whatever holiday came next.

Maybe one day Alice would ask me about our daddy, beg me to tell her why we left him behind when we moved to Ohio. She'd been spared seeing him at his worst, but she was so little, she might also forget the good times.

One day when Alice was old enough to understand, I'd tell her about how he drove a hundred miles each way to get the doll she wanted for her birthday. And how he sat with her on those little chairs at Sunday school until she told him she wasn't scared anymore and he could go sit with Mama in the church.

Don't you remember, Alice, I'd remind her, *how when we got sick Daddy came home at lunchtime with a stack of comic books and pints of ice cream? And how he let us eat straight out of the cartons?*

I gazed at my baby sister; envy filled my heart. Some days I wished I was four years old and didn't have to worry about anything.

"Sarah Jane, come look." Alice clapped her hands. "I finished the puzzle. All by myself."

"Good for you, Alice." I was trying to think up something else for her to do when the office door swished open and Mama stepped into the room.

"I got myself a job."

Henry stood and did a little bow. "You must be Mrs. Otis. I'm Henry Buckner, Sweetwater Motel handyman and jigsaw-puzzle consultant."

Mama shook his hand. "Pleased to meet you. I hope my girls haven't been any trouble."

"They're good company."

Alice jumped up from her chair. "Did you get me a cherry sucker?"

"Something better," said Mama. "I got you a future." She turned to me. "It's going to be smooth sailing from now on, Sarah Jane. I can feel it in my bones."

"That's real good, Mama."

A job meant we were staying. A job meant there was no chance she'd try to work things out with Daddy. I gazed out the window searching the road for Daddy's Buick. *If you're coming, Daddy, you'd better hurry up.*

I am asking you nicely, God, please let me make some friends at school. If you eat lunch alone, you might as well have LOSER written on your forehead. Please, please, please, let me make a friend. Someone cool. Someone who won't drop me like a hot potato if she finds out I live in a motel.

CHAPTER 12

A Girl Named Fred

MAMA'S JOB was both a blessing and a curse. She started working as an assistant teacher at Little Lambs Daycare Center the very next Monday, two days before the start of school.

Little Lambs was close enough to the motel to walk to if I had an emergency and needed to see her. The good news was she could keep Alice with her; the bad news was she had to be to work by seven in the morning, so she wouldn't be able to drive me to school.

"You'll have to take the bus, Sarah Jane." She pointed to a street on the bus schedule. "It's a two-minute walk."

A Girl Named Fred

"But, Mama, the kids who wait there will want to know where I live."

"Just say you live down the road a piece."

"They're going to figure out I live at a motel. By first period everyone else at school will know. 'She's the poor girl who lives in the motel,' they'll say, and no one will want to come near me. I'll have to eat lunch alone for the rest of my life."

"Stop being so melodramatic. I don't have time for this. I bet by the end of the day you'll have lots of new friends. Now, help Alice get dressed, or I'm going to be late for work."

I did as she asked, my hands shaking from anger as I buttoned Alice's overalls. How could Mama expect me to make friends with those kids? Did she really think their parents would let them hang out with a girl who lived in a motel?

With Mama and Alice at Little Lambs, and school not opening until Wednesday, I was on my own. Mrs. Sweetwater kept me busy for the next two days, or I might have bitten off the ends of my fingers with worry. I had to come up with a plan to get to school without taking the bus.

I helped Mrs. Sweetwater with the motel chores, stripping the beds and cleaning the bathrooms, disgusting enough to make me gag.

Mrs. Sweetwater carried a portable CD player from room to room so we could listen to music while we worked. She told me it was Big Band music from the forties. She played it real loud so she could hear it over the noise of the vacuum cleaner. She'd shimmy her hips as she propelled the vacuum across the carpet.

I don't think any of the people who stayed in those motel rooms had ever learned to pick up after themselves. They left empty beer cans, petrified pizza, and ashtrays filled with stinky cigarette butts. Some people even forgot underwear that we found when we cleaned under the beds.

Mama said if we helped with the motel chores, Mrs. Sweetwater would let us stay there for almost nothing. The more we saved from what Mama made at her job at the daycare center, the faster we'd get our own place.

Mrs. Sweetwater handed me a cold drink and a ten-dollar bill when I returned from carrying the last of the trash to the Dumpster.

"You don't have to pay me," I said as I held out the money to her.

"Go ahead and take it. It's your tip. Everyone deserves a tip when they do such a good job."

"Mama wouldn't like me to take it on account of you being nice and giving us such a good deal on the rooms."

She smiled and pressed the bill into my hand. "Nice has nothing to do with it. You earned this, Sarah Jane. Besides, a girl needs to have some mad money."

"What's mad money?"

She played with her dangly earrings. "Oh, you know, a bit of cash so you can buy yourself a bauble or two. Maybe one day your mother will let me take you to the mall and we can shop till we drop." She laughed and gave my hand a squeeze. "We could have a girls' day out."

"My grandma Emma used to take me shopping. We liked to try on fancy hats at Mitchell's Department Store and eat barbecue at Jack's Corral."

"You must miss her."

I knew if I started talking about Grandma Emma and back home, I'd start bawling my eyes out. "Thanks for the tip," I said, and slipped the money into my pocket. "I have to go now."

School started on Wednesday. Mama and Alice left the motel at quarter to seven. I sat at the kitchen table eating a bowl of cereal and reading the list Mama'd left me.

Before School
Fix your lunch
Sneakers for gym
Feed Mabel
Clean litter box

After School
Motel chores
Do laundry
Do your homework
Start dinner

I thought about going back to bed and pretending to be sick. I did feel sick to my stomach, and I had a headache. This was going to be the worst day of my life.

The bus didn't come for another hour. I was getting dressed when I had a brainstorm. Maybe no one would have to know where I lived after all. I had two strong legs and plenty of time. I could walk to school.

I put on a red T-shirt and the best pair of jeans I owned, and pulled on my red boots. My hair didn't look too bad. I fixed the sides with a couple of barrettes. After I fed Mabel and kissed her good-bye, I grabbed my backpack and headed out the door.

Henry stood in front of the office cleaning the window. "You're looking mighty spiffy," he said.

"Thank you." I waved good-bye. I didn't have time for a long conversation.

"First day of school?"

"Yes, I have to go. I don't want to miss the bus."

He checked his watch. "Kind of early for the bus."

"I don't like to rush."

He waved a rag at me. "You have a nice day."

"I will." I walked toward the road, wondering if he believed me.

I turned right at the end of the drive, then backtracked and walked quickly in the other direction. I needed to avoid kids waiting at their bus stops, so I cut through a few backyards. A poodle wearing a red bow on its head charged at me from behind a picnic table.

"Aren't you late for a dog show?" I shouted at the beast.

The doors to the school didn't open until eight o'clock. I bided my time sitting on a rock in a wooded area across from the school where I could wait and watch. I'd have to remember to bring something to sit on so I wouldn't get my clothes dirty, and a book to read.

Plop, plop. Just what I needed, rain. And me without an umbrella. I covered my head with my backpack.

After a half hour, the first school bus pulled up to the front door. Dozens of kids swarmed into the school, yelling to each other, happy to see their friends.

I moved quickly, careful to blend in with the

crowd of kids jostling each other as they squeezed through the doors. It took me a few minutes to find my locker. I checked the letter I'd received the week before to make sure I had the right one.

"You look like a drowned rat."

The girl who spoke had the locker next to mine. She gave me the once-over. She wasn't much taller than Alice.

"I got caught in the rain."

"Hey, you've got a Southern accent. Where'd you walk from, Texas?"

"I missed the bus." Not that it was any of her business. My locker door would not budge. I tried wiggling, kicking, and twisting, but it was jammed tighter than a door in August.

"Stand back," said my nosy neighbor before she slipped a ruler along the edge of my locker and pried it open with her fingers.

"Thanks." I tried not to stare at her, but she was really small. She barely came up to my armpits.

"Yeah, whatever. At least these little fingers are good for something."

"My name is Sarah Jane Otis."

She stared at me.

"I'm new."

"So?" She slammed her locker shut and left me wondering who she was and what I had done to make her hate me in less than two minutes.

"I'll see you later." I called after her. I almost added that I was *really* new, hoping that would explain why I was so clueless, but she already thought I was weird, so I shut up.

The bell rang. A metallic slam of locker doors vibrated through the halls. Hundreds of kids filled the hallway, elbowing their way to class.

I cowered near a doorway, unsure which way to move.

"Oh, come on." She of the little fingers was back and she had me by the arm.

I still couldn't move.

"I'm not trying to kidnap you. My name is Fred. That's short for Fredericka. Now that we've been properly introduced, tell me where your homeroom is and I'll take you there."

I showed her my schedule, and without another word she escorted me to room 109.

"You're lucky I don't charge for baby-sitting you. From now on, Sarah J., you're on your own. Watch out for Tracey and Deena; those girls make you believe in witches. And ignore Doug. He's a jerk, but he's not smart enough to do much damage. That's all the free advice you're getting from me."

She slipped into a seat at the back of the room. I found an empty desk near the window. Our homeroom teacher, Mr. Roberts, bounded into the room.

"Good morning, everyone. Are you ready for a great year?"

Mr. Roberts's thin lips stretched into a smile. I wanted to believe him when he told us all we had to do was work hard and show school spirit, and it would be our best school year ever.

I wanted to believe.

I had gym first period, which meant I'd have bad hair and stink for the rest of the day. Our teacher, Mr. Bosco, made us line up on the red line. He wore his hair in a military crew cut and had the thick, muscular neck of a Clydesdale horse.

As soon as I saw all the other kids in gym shoes, I remembered I'd left my sneakers back at the motel.

"Line up on the red line." Mr. Bosco paced in front of us, clipboard in hand, a drill sergeant inspecting his troops.

"You must be a cowgirl." He pointed to my red boots.

"I forgot my sneakers," I said.

He made a mark next to my name and moved on to a tall, skinny boy named Arthur Proctor, who had a bad case of pimples. He wore high-tops the size of mailboxes.

A boy named Doug whispered out of the side of his mouth. "You'll be doing push-ups until midnight."

I turned in time to see a smirk cross his face.

"Miss Otis, if you're not too busy, might I have your undivided attention." Mr. Bosco had eyes on the side of his head.

He explained we would learn more than how to play games in his class. "In my class, you will learn Bosco's Rules of Life. Every week you will learn a new rule. If you're quick learners, you may get two rules a week."

He claimed anyone who learned to live by his rules would hold the key to success. I wished he'd tell us how to make a friend by lunchtime.

"Write this down," he said, and then waited while we scrambled for paper and pencil. "Rule Number One: Wear comfortable shoes appropriate for the task at hand."

My first day of class and I'd already managed to break Rule Number One. Since I couldn't clomp around the gym in my boots and scuff up the polished floors, I got to inventory the supply closet, doing the "important" job of counting volleyballs and badminton birdies. The rest of the kids, who remembered Rule Number One, played dodgeball.

Most of the boys attacked Arthur, an easy target who tripped over his own feet. He flinched as the ball flew at his cranelike legs, and he didn't have the reflexes to block it with his hands.

After gym, a few of the girls asked me if I was new, but no one seemed interested in where I lived.

"I like your boots," said a girl named Tiffany. She changed from her gym shoes to a pair of leather clogs.

"Thanks. I like your shoes." I wished I could think of something interesting to say.

"Don't let Bosco get to you. He's all talk."

"He made a mark next to my name."

Tiffany laughed and tossed her long blond hair "My sister had him for gym. She said he makes a mark next to someone's name every day, but he never does anything about it. Everyone gets a B in his class, unless you're a star athlete— then you get an A."

"Did your sister learn Bosco's rules of life?"

"Yeah, she gave me the list, so I was prepared."

It wouldn't hurt to be ready for the next class. "What's Rule Number Two?"

Tiffany leaned in close and smiled. "Don't eat anything that will give you gas before a big game."

Tomorrow we get our gym uniforms. White tops and green shorts. Mama could have used the money for food, but she acted as if it was okay, as if having what I needed for school was as important as eating.

CHAPTER 13

Just Desserts

FRED STOOD at the end of the lunch line, pushing her tray along the metal ledge with one hand, clutching money with the other. It was a relief to see someone I knew.

"You got anything good?" She eyed my brown paper bag.

"Peanut-butter-and-jelly and a banana."

"That's a little kid's lunch."

"I was in a hurry this morning."

"Yeah, right. You missed the bus." She rolled her eyes at me.

"I did miss the bus."

She moved closer. "I don't give a darn if you hopped all the way to school like a kangaroo. But if you missed the bus and had to walk, you would have been late to school. But you got here before the buses."

"I did not."

Fred's eyes bored into mine as if she were reading my mind. "Sarah J., I know you're lying. Do you want to know how I know?"

"Okay. Tell me." I said this as if it were a dare.

"Because I saw you walk out of the woods. That's why you were soaked when you came into school."

My face grew warm. I wanted to turn and run away, but a line had formed behind me.

"Hey, don't get all embarrassed because I caught you in your lie. I like liars. At least you know not to believe anything they say. It's the kids who act all goody-goody you can't trust. They tell you the truth one minute and lie the next."

We moved along the line. I picked up a carton of milk. Fred bought the school lunch, which was spaghetti and meatballs. Or I should say, spaghetti and meat*ball*.

"My mom thinks I'll grow faster if I eat a hot lunch." She looked down at herself and laughed, but she wasn't smiling. "Maybe there's something in this food that's shrinking me."

She handed the cashier her money. "I'm taking an ice cream," she said.

I paid for my milk. Fred reached into the cooler chest for an ice-cream sandwich. She pulled out two, slipping one under the sleeve of her jean jacket. It happened quickly, in one fluid motion, as if she'd done it before.

"Come on," she said, her voice a growl. I stood still, my mouth agape. "Sarah J., remind me not to use you to drive the getaway car when I rob a bank."

Fred walked behind me, prodding me with her knee to get me moving. I figured that was her way of inviting me to eat lunch with her. She found a table near the windows that looked out on a courtyard.

"Sit down and stop looking so guilty. You didn't steal anything." She let the extra ice cream slip from her sleeve and drop in front of me.

I didn't know what to do. How could I eat the ice cream? I didn't pay for it. Fred didn't pay for it. It was wrong.

We sat across from Tracey and Deena, the girls Fred had warned me about. They wore the same shade of teal-blue eye shadow. Tracey dropped her change on her tray, but ignored her lunch. The two of them concentrated on the boys who walked past, rating them from one to ten.

Arthur Proctor, the dodgeball victim from gym, paused to look for a place to sit, blocking their view. Every time he found an empty seat, the kids at the table told him the seat was saved, or piled their stuff on the space.

Tracey and Deena watched Arthur walk away. "Zero," they said at the same time, before collapsing with laughter.

Arthur tried a few more tables, each time getting rejected. He finally gave up and went outside to the courtyard, where he sat on a bench and ate his lunch. He threw bread crusts to a bird that hovered at his feet.

Fred leaned over her plate, sucking up the spaghetti, loud enough to get Tracey's and Deena's attention.

Tracey made a gagging sound. "That is so gross." Deena screwed up her face.

Fred shoved the whole meatball into her mouth, then proceeded to chew it with her mouth open, leaning toward Tracey and Deena so they got a good view.

"Want some?" asked Fred, spraying specks of meat in their direction.

They rolled their eyes, turned their backs to us, and went back to boy watching.

I ate my sandwich slowly, chewing each bite twenty times, hoping to make it last to the end of the lunch period so I wouldn't have time to eat the ice cream.

Fred ate the last strand of spaghetti, sat back, and belched. "There's only five minutes left. Let's eat our ice cream."

She shoved my unfinished peanut butter sandwich to the side, then placed the ice-cream sandwich squarely in front of me. I stared at it, waiting for a sign of what to do.

"Sarah J., you'll never get anywhere in life if you're indecisive. Look at me. If I want something, I go for it."

Fred inched her fingers across the table under cover of her jacket. While Tracey and Deena ogled a redheaded boy, she slipped the three one-dollar bills that lay on Tracey's tray under her jacket. In one motion, she scooped up the jacket, the money wrapped inside.

The redheaded boy asked Tracey and Deena if they wanted to walk to class together. They jumped from their seats, grabbed their stuff, and left.

I wondered how rich you'd have to be not to miss three dollars. Three dollars would buy enough boxes of macaroni-and-cheese to feed Mama, Alice, and me for days.

"She didn't even miss her money," I said to Fred.

Fred unwrapped my ice cream, flattening the paper against the table. "The bell's going to ring in a minute."

I picked up the ice-cream sandwich and took a bite. I expected it to be bitter, as if Fred's stealing it could spoil its taste. It melted on my tongue, cold and sweet.

The bell rang. I remained in my seat, eating my ice cream slowly, savoring its sweetness, letting it comfort me.

Thanks for giving me someone to eat lunch with at school, God. She's small and she's bossy, but it's okay, because I think she likes me.

CHAPTER 14

"I Turn the Pages"

I SAID MY SILENT prayer over a dinner of fish sticks and macaroni and cheese from a box. I didn't mention the ice cream to God. Or the money Fred had stolen.

Mama asked how my day went.

"Pretty good," I answered.

She smiled at me and wiped cheese from Alice's chin. "Make any friends?"

"My locker got stuck and a girl helped me get it open. She's in my homeroom and my history class and we sat together at lunch."

Arthur Proctor was also in my history class, but he was so quiet, I didn't notice him until the bell rang and he jumped from his seat and ran out of the room.

"Didn't I tell you you'd make friends? See there, Sarah Jane, you were worrying for nothing. What's your friend's name?"

"Fred, that's short for Fredericka. She's not much bigger than Alice."

Alice's mouth opened wide. A half-chewed piece of fish stick fell out. "I want to see her," she said.

"Alice, she's not a freak or anything. She's just small. She said it's a medical condition."

"Is she a midget?" asked Alice

"Little people," said Mama. "I read in a magazine that's what they like to be called."

"No, I don't think she's a little person. Her doctor told her she might get to be four and a half feet tall."

"Well, it doesn't matter, as long as she's a nice girl. Having a friend makes all the difference." Mama shoveled more macaroni on my plate.

"I still want to see her." Alice took the last fish stick and crammed it into her mouth.

Mama stood in the open doorway, smoking

her after-dinner cigarette. "You should ask your new friend over while the weather is warm enough to use the pool."

"I think she's busy all the time."

"Suit yourself," said Mama. She came inside, wiped Alice's hands with a paper napkin, and put away the tartar sauce. "I'm beat from chasing little kids all day. Stack the dishes in the sink for me while I give Alice her bath."

It would be fun to have someone besides Alice to swim with, but Fred might change her mind about eating lunch with me if she found out I lived at a motel. She was the only friend I had, so I couldn't take the chance.

I wondered if the incident at lunch was a one-time occurrence, something Fred had done to impress me, like the way Alice used to turn cartwheels when we had company.

Mama says people judge you by the company you keep. Being the new girl, they might think I was a bad influence on Fred, the instigator who led her into a life of crime. "What did you expect," they'd say, "from a trashy girl who lives in a motel?"

After I wiped down the counters, I jammed my sneakers into my backpack so I wouldn't forget them again.

Alice sat up in bed, a pile of picture books resting on her legs. "Mama said you have to read to me."

"I don't have to do anything." Alice always picked the same book. "Okay, but just one," I said.

I read the words slowly, giving Alice a chance to look at the pictures.

"I turn the pages," she said, same as always. Ever since the time she had caught me skipping pages, she insisted on doing the turning.

"Alice, remember how Daddy used to bring us comic books when we got sick?"

She looked up at me, her eyes wide. "Yeah, and we got to eat ice cream out of the carton."

"That's right, Alice. We ate straight out of the carton."

She shook her head in agreement, grasped the corner of the next page, fingering it to make sure it was not two, and flipped it over.

I can't believe this is only the second day of school. The little sleep I got was filled with dreams of being arrested for eating stolen ice cream. "Take her straight to jail!" screamed the cafeteria ladies, as a police officer handcuffed me in front of Tracey and Deena. Fred pretended she didn't know me. I woke up exhausted. The first thing I did was examine my wrists for red marks. I will try to do better today, God. I've got my sneakers for gym and enough food to keep me busy for the whole lunch period. No matter what Fred says, I will eat only what's mine.

CHAPTER 15

A Knight in High-Tops

I PACKED A lunch of hard-boiled eggs, a hunk of cheddar cheese, an apple, and a stack of graham crackers. Nothing babyish about hard-boiled eggs. At the last minute, I grabbed a book to read while I waited in the woods for the buses to arrive. I still hadn't figured out what I'd do when the weather turned cold, but that day I had bigger things to worry about.

"What did you bring for lunch?" Fred stretched to place a folder on the top shelf of her locker. Her sweatshirt rose up. "Let me guess, peanut butter and jelly?"

"No, hard-boiled eggs."

"Wow, that's exciting."

Just what I needed first thing in the morning, a food critic. I was trying to think of something witty to zing at her when I noticed that the back waistband of her jeans had elastic, like the little-kids' pants Alice wore.

Fred caught me staring. "Why don't you take a picture? It will last longer." She tugged her sweatshirt, slammed her locker shut, and headed off to homeroom.

Oh boy, I'd offended my one and only friend. "I've got money," I shouted after her. "I'll treat you to ice cream today."

I should have been saving the "mad" money I got from Mrs. Sweetwater for something important, like furniture for our new apartment. But I didn't want to have to eat lunch alone with the birds.

Fred ignored me during homeroom. I trudged to gym, wondering what Mr. Bosco had planned. He handed out our gym uniforms, gave us four minutes to change into them and get to our places on the red line. He made a big show of noticing my sneakers.

"All right, Cowgirl. Glad to see you remembered Rule Number One."

Someone down the line snickered. I stared straight ahead.

Mr. Bosco finished taking attendance. "I always enjoy seeing everyone in their new uniforms. Now, for Rule Number Two."

I waited for him to tell us the one about not eating anything that would cause gas before a big game.

"Since Rule Number Two seems to cause the less mature people in my class to make rude noises for the rest of the period, I've come up with a new Rule Number Two. File this away for later use." He tapped his forehead with his index finger. "At the end of the day, go home."

Doug raised his hand. "Where else are you going to go?" he asked.

Mr. Bosco smiled. "Think about it."

The other gym teacher, Ms. Albanese, a tall, skinny lady who wore fancy warm-up suits, came by to talk to Mr. Bosco about supplies. He let us decide what we wanted to do. The majority of the kids voted to play dodgeball.

Arthur sighed and rolled his eyes. "I'm dead."

Doug Baxter, a boy half the height of Arthur and twice the width, a bulldog in gym shorts, got control of the ball. He decided to spare Arthur and go after me.

I ran as fast as I could to the other end of the gym. I attempted to zigzag. My old sneakers, treadless as bald tires, slipped on the polished wood floor. I landed with a thud on my rear, skinning my elbow in the crash.

Mr. Bosco and Ms. Albanese stood at the other end of the gym deep in conversation, their backs to us. Terminator Doug approached, a wide smile smeared across his face.

He raised the ball, ready to bounce it off my head. Arthur stepped between us. He took the ball hard in his stomach, which knocked the wind out of him and sent him crashing to the floor.

When he tried to stand, Doug smashed him again with the ball. Arthur stopped trying to get up and lay still, shielding his head with his arms.

I jumped to my feet, shoved Doug out of the way and offered my hand to Arthur. The scene reminded me of the night I had discovered

Mama sprawled on the kitchen floor, my daddy standing over her.

"Get up!" I yelled at Arthur. "Don't let him do this to you."

Doug squawked and did the chicken dance.

Mr. Bosco turned to see what all the commotion was about. Arthur sat up, gulping air.

"Get with it, Proctor. There are no time-outs in dodgeball." Mr. Bosco turned his attention back to Ms. Albanese.

I appreciated being spared having my brain tossed inside my head like a Jell-O salad in a mold, but Arthur's act of chivalry gave the boys more ammunition to use against him. And me.

"Arthur loves the cowgirl!" they shouted like some kind of team cheer.

I glared at Arthur. "Why didn't you mind your own business? I don't need a boy to protect me. I can take care of myself."

Doug and his friends surrounded Arthur, nudging him with their sneakers and calling him Prince of Pimples and Chief Big Feet.

Why did Arthur let those boys treat him that way? Didn't he have any pride?

Mr. Bosco, who looked as if he were trying to make a love connection with Ms. Albanese, finally got the idea that his class was out of control.

He threw down his clipboard and blew his whistle. "The party's over. Everybody, ten laps around the gym. And no cutting corners."

"Nice going, Pimple Man," Doug said to Arthur as he passed him near the basketball hoop.

I wanted to tell Doug to shut up and remind him that he was the one who had started the trouble, but I kept my mouth shut and kept running.

Arthur plodded along. He could have taken his skinny legs to court and sued them for lack of support.

The other kids passed him, trying to be the first to finish and be excused to go to the locker rooms. Without trying, I caught up to him, almost stepping on his heels.

I pulled to the left and moved past him, my eyes straight ahead. "I'm sorry, Sarah Jane," he said in a pleading voice. I pretended not to hear.

Thanks to blabbermouth Doug, most of the seventh-grade class, including Fred, knew by lunchtime about Arthur trying to rescue me.

"Ignore them," said Fred, as we neared a table of Neanderthal boys who made kissing noises and told me to say hi to Arthur.

One of them, a boy named Butch, whose upper lip showed signs of a mustache, told me to be careful or I might catch Arthur's pimples.

"They're jerks." Fred moved closer to their table, knocking over Butch's opened bottle of juice with her elbow, splattering the red liquid on his pants.

"You are so dead, Midget Girl!" he screamed at her.

She flipped him the finger, then found us a spot near the windows, same as usual. And same as usual, Arthur sat outside by himself, feeding bread crusts to the birds.

Seeing him so alone made me feel sorry for him again. Sorry he had such big feet, sorry he had the worst case of pimples I had ever seen. But why did he have to protect me from Doug? I could take care of myself, and I would rather have lost a few hundred brain cells from getting pummeled with a ball than be known as Arthur Proctor's girlfriend.

"Don't waste your time worrying about Arthur," said Fred. "He practically wears a Kick Me sign on his back." She picked up the hamburger from her tray and took a huge bite.

"What do you mean?"

"Look at him." She pointed outside to Arthur. He leaned toward the ground, deep in conversation with the birds. "Doug and those other jerks have been picking on him forever, and he never does anything to defend himself."

"He tried to protect me."

"Yeah, but from what I heard, all he did was stand there and let Doug use him for target practice. Either he's a wimp or he's been reading too many books about Gandhi."

"You mean that Indian man who believed in peace through nonviolence?"

"Whatever. All I know is you need to keep your gloves on, and if there's going to be a fight you'd better throw the first punch."

"Doesn't that make you as bad as Doug?"

"You're missing the point, Sarah J. Doug's a

bully. And bullies pick on people who lie down like doormats and take it. You don't see Doug messing with me, and I'm half his size."

I wondered where her courage came from—if you were born with it or learned it to survive.

Fred nudged me with her elbow. "By the way, I figured you worked up an appetite running laps in gym so I got you something extra to eat." She slipped a hamburger wrapped in a napkin from her backpack.

How did she do it? *Courageous* wasn't a strong enough word to describe Fred. The girl was fearless.

"Eat up." She handed the burger to me.

The warm burger tasted better than the hard-boiled eggs I'd brought from home. I gobbled it down as I watched Arthur come inside. He cut a wide berth around Doug's table and left the cafeteria.

Doug hooted at Arthur, then turned and stared at me. I pretended to pick my nose and flick it at him.

Fred did the same. "Hey, Sarah J. Maybe you're not as hopeless as I thought."

What makes some people so mean, God? Did you put that cruelty in their hearts? And is it really true that the meek shall inherit the earth? If it is, then Arthur Proctor's going to be a big property owner one day. But unless he learns to stand up for himself, Doug will take it away from him quicker than you can do the chicken dance.

CHAPTER 16

Five-Finger Discount

OUR WEEKS after the start of school, I got up extra early so I could have a heart-to-heart with Mama. I even made her coffee and had it waiting for her in the kitchen.

"Mama, we have to talk."

She sighed. "Can't this wait until tonight?"

"No, you have to look at this." I placed the paper with the grid on the table and smoothed its edges.

"What's this?" She sipped her coffee.

"Remember the office lady said we had six weeks to get our own place?"

"Yes, I remember."

"And she said if we didn't have a real address

162

in six weeks we'd have to pay tuition. Three thousand dollars." I pointed to the boxes, twenty-eight of them checked off. "We have only fourteen days left."

"This *is* a real address." She reached out and touched the wall. "Feels real to me."

"But, Mama . . ."

"Stop your worrying. I know what that lady said, but she was wrong. I talked to someone at social services, and they said we don't have to pay for you to go to that school even if we live at a motel."

"Are you sure?"

"It's the law, they have to take you."

They had to take me, as if I were a stray animal that needed a home. "It will be on my permanent record that I lived at the Sweetwater Motel."

She rolled her eyes at me. "Don't be a drama queen. Besides, nothing is ever permanent. Now, hurry up and get ready for school."

I stomped into the bathroom. A spider ran across the floor. Living at the motel sure felt permanent to me. I feared I'd be sharing a room with Alice for the rest of our lives, with Mama sleeping on the pullout sofa.

So far, no one at school knew where I lived. Mostly because I kept to myself, except for hanging out with Fred. She'd stopped stealing me ice cream and moved up the food chain to entrées, pocketing an extra hamburger or hot dog for me when the cafeteria lady turned her back. I ate everything she took. It was better than eating peanut-butter sandwiches every day.

Alice pounded on the bathroom door. "I have to go!" she yelled. I let her in and went to get dressed.

Locking the bedroom door behind me, I pulled my suitcase from under the bed and removed my new blouse, the one Fred had stolen for me the last time we went to the mall.

We went to the movies on Saturday afternoons. Fred said it was the best time to go because the lobby was always crowded with screaming kids, which made it easy for us to sneak by the ticket taker.

At first I was scared someone would grab me by the collar and ask to see my ticket, but Fred had an answer for everything.

"If someone stops you, say your mom has the

tickets and she's in the ladies' room because she has diarrhea."

The more we did it, the easier it got. Fred used the money from her mom to buy us popcorn and drinks.

After the movies, we'd walk around the mall and cruise the shops. "Pick out something you like," Fred said one day as she pointed to a rack of clothes in the junior department.

"I don't have any money with me."

"So what? Pick out a shirt. Didn't you say you could use a new one?"

"I guess." We looked through some racks. I pretended to not like anything. Then I saw it, the most perfect blouse. Dark blue cotton with long sleeves, embroidered with small red and white flowers around the neck.

"Try it on." Fred grabbed it and pushed it at me.

A saleslady stood at the cash register waiting on two other girls. She ignored us.

I took the blouse into a dressing room and tried it on. Fred knocked on the door. "Let me see how it looks."

I opened the door and struck a pose. "I like it. It looks good with these jeans and my red boots."

"You should definitely get it."

I checked the price tag. It cost three times as much as the mad money I had hidden in my closet. "Not today."

"It might not be here when you come back." Fred opened her purse and removed a paper bag labeled with the name of the store.

"Where did you get that?"

"I always save bags from stores that I like. It makes it easier."

"Easier for what?" As if I didn't know where this was headed.

Fred stepped into my dressing room and closed the door. "Take off the shirt, fold it up real small and put it in the bag."

"Turn around while I change." I removed the embroidered shirt and put my old shirt back on. "I can't do this."

"Oh, give it to me." Fred folded the shirt until it fit neatly into the bag.

Stepping from the dressing room, we paused

at the opening to the teen department. The saleslady continued to chat with some customers.

My heart raced as we got on the escalator. A man in a suit stood at the bottom, as if he were waiting for us.

"Maybe there was a camera in the dressing room," I whispered to Fred.

"Zip it."

The man in the suit watched us. My dream was coming true. At any moment he'd whip out handcuffs. I turned and retreated, running up the escalator, almost knocking over a lady carrying two shopping bags.

Fred followed me. "What do you think you're doing?"

"That man," I said, gasping for breath.

"What man?"

I turned in time to see the man in the suit greet the lady with the shopping bags. He took the bags from her and they walked off together.

"I thought he was a store detective." I couldn't stop shaking.

Fred pulled me over to a stool set next to a makeup counter. "Sit down and chill."

"It's getting late. Your mama's going to be waiting for us."

She glanced at her watch. "Okay, let's go, but I'll carry the bag so you won't freak out."

"What if someone suspects?"

"You drop the bag and run. They can't do anything to you unless you leave the store with the stuff. If they stop you in here, just say you were going to pay for it."

"What about the bag? Why would it be in a bag if you were going to pay for it?"

Fred gave me a patient smile. "Then I'll tell them that I bring my own bags when I shop to conserve paper."

"Fred, did you ever think about using your great mind for something legal?"

"Ha-ha, very funny. Now, wipe that guilty look off your face. And do you think you can walk through the store without freaking out and confessing to the first person you see?"

I studied my face in the mirror on the counter. "Okay, I'm ready."

"You be the lookout. I'll carry the bag."

Fred and her mom dropped me off a few

blocks from the motel, same as usual. I always used the excuse that I had to pick up something for Mama at the market.

I slipped the bag inside my shirt and hid it from Mama in my suitcase under the bed, along with the new jeans, the belt, and the makeup Fred had stolen for me. Since I dressed after Mama left for work and changed into my old clothes before she came home, it was easy to do.

The more I lied, the easier it got. Living in a place where no one really knew who we were, it became simple to reinvent myself. Some days I felt as if we were in one of those witness protection programs. We'd left everything behind except our names.

Honor thy mother and father. That's what they used to teach us in Sunday school, God. How can I respect my daddy after what he did to us? And I'm not feeling particularly kindly toward Mama, either.

CHAPTER 17
Skipping School

MAMA HAD HER secrets too. I read a letter she'd hidden in her underwear drawer. I'd seen her put it there when she thought I was asleep. The letter came on thick stationery from a lawyer telling her he had filed papers so she could get a divorce from Daddy.

My hands trembled with the effort it took to refrain from tearing the letter to bits. How could she go ahead and divorce Daddy without saying a word to me?

Well, let her be that way. I didn't need her anymore, the way Alice did. I could take care of myself. I was glad she left early for work. It gave me a chance to be alone, so I could eat my breakfast in peace without the sound of Alice's cartoon shows blaring and Mama nagging at me.

One morning as I posed in front of the mirror, slicking on the lip gloss Fred had gotten me from the drugstore, the phone rang. We didn't get many calls, so I figured it was Mama telling me to chip the dried ketchup off the kitchen table or do some other exciting chore.

"Hello," I said. I repeated the word a second and third time. Someone took a quick breath; I heard a click and the phone went dead.

I wondered if I should call Little Lambs and tell Mama we'd gotten another hang-up call. We'd had three that week, but Alice had grabbed the phone the other times, and we figured maybe it was someone selling something and they didn't want to talk to a little kid. After those calls, Mama forbade Alice to pick up the phone.

"Do you think it's Daddy?" I'd asked Mama when Alice was out of earshot. "Do you think he's found us?"

"If that was him, he'd be here by now, breaking down our door. I'll bet you a million dollars he's working at the plant every day

172

and getting drunk every night, same as always."

She seemed to regret saying this, because she told me she was joking, and I shouldn't worry because Daddy would never figure we'd be living in a motel in Dublin, Ohio.

That morning, alone in the living room, I stared at the phone. If Mama were right, Daddy would be at work. I knew the number by heart.

I dialed and waited. A woman answered on the second ring. I told her I needed to speak to Mr. Otis, making it sound official.

She put me on hold. I was about to hang up when someone picked up the receiver.

"Hello."

More than a thousand miles from home, my daddy's voice came through the phone line loud and clear. I placed my hand over the mouthpiece, and held my breath.

"Hello, who is this?"

It's Sarah Jane. I said the words in my head. If he really loved me, if he missed me, wouldn't he know it was me?

"Becky, is this you?"

He thought it was Mama calling him up.

173

"Darling, is it you?"

Darling. He called her *darling.* "It's Sarah Jane." It took two beats of my heart before I realized I'd whispered my name into the phone. Said it loud enough for him to hear.

"Sarah Jane, where are you, baby? Are you all right?"

"I'm okay."

"I miss you," he said, and I could tell he meant it.

"I have to go," I said.

"Please don't hang up. Just tell me if you're okay. You're not hurt are you?"

"No, I'm okay. Mama and Alice are okay too."

"You sound so far away. Are you in Florida? Your mama always said she'd like to live in Florida."

I was about to say no, we weren't in Florida, when I realized what he was doing. "I have to go, Daddy."

"Sarah Jane. I'm real sorry for what happened. I stopped drinking and everything. Is your mama there? Let me talk to her."

"She's not here. I'm going to hang up now."

"Give me your number so I can call you back and talk to you and Alice. A man should at least be able to talk to his kids."

"I can't. Mama wouldn't like it."

"I miss you, baby girl. Tell your mama I'm a changed man. Come home so we can be a family again. I promise you on a stack of bibles, I won't ever lay a hand on either of you again."

I touched the scar on my cheek. "Bye, Daddy."

"Do you miss me even a little bit?"

"Yes, Daddy, I miss you."

I hung up the phone before he could make any more promises. Before I started to believe his words.

I wanted to believe him. It would make things so easy if we could go home. Maybe Mama would change her mind about the divorce if she knew he had stopped drinking.

What Daddy had done was wrong. No one had the right to hurt another person. And he had hurt us real bad. On the outside where it showed, and on the inside in our hearts. Mama told me she could never forgive him for killing her spirit, for taking away her trust.

I wanted to hate him. But he was my daddy, the only one I had. And he missed me.

Sweat ran down my sides. Should I call Mama and tell her what I'd done?

Someone knocked at our door. My brain told me there was no way Daddy could have gotten from Georgia to Ohio in five minutes, but all the same, I tiptoed to the living room and peeked through the curtains. Henry stood outside holding a brown paper sack in his arms. My hand trembled as I unlocked the door and slid the chain latch from its hook.

Henry smiled and tipped his head. "Hope I didn't catch you at a bad time."

"Mama and Alice already left for daycare."

"I thought you might want some of these apples. I work part-time at a horse farm and they have an orchard full of apple trees. They let me take what I want."

"Thank you," I said.

He offered me the bag, but my arms remained frozen at my sides.

"Anything wrong, Sarah Jane?" Henry placed the bag of apples inside the door. "Everything okay?"

I burst out crying. Once I got going, I couldn't stop. I felt guilty for missing Daddy. How could I be so disloyal? Mama was doing the best she could. This couldn't be easy for her.

Henry reached around me, closed our door, and locked it with his master key. Without a word, he took me by the hand and led me to the office and to Mrs. Sweetwater, who wrapped me in her soft arms and held me to her until my tears dried up and my sobs turned to hiccups.

She brewed me a cup of green tea, tucked me into her favorite chair, and covered me with a yellow blanket. I sipped my tea. Its scent reminded me of eating out in Chinese restaurants. Mrs. Sweetwater settled into a chair pulled close to mine and took up her knitting. She turned rose-colored yarn into a fancy pattern, never dropping a stitch even when she looked up from her work to smile at me.

She never asked what was wrong. And she didn't call Mama. She just let me be.

When it got to be eight o'clock, she called the school and told someone in the office that Sarah Jane Otis wouldn't be in today, that she was not feeling well.

When I woke from a nap, my teacup was gone. The soft blanket was tucked under my chin; my hands lay safe beneath the cover.

I heard Henry and Mrs. Sweetwater speaking softly in the kitchen. They stopped talking when they noticed me standing in the doorway.

Mrs. Sweetwater lay down her hand of cards. "Are you hungry, sweet girl?"

I looked at the clock hanging above the sink. "It's almost noon."

"You were sleeping like a baby," said Henry. "Muriel and I are on our hundredth game of gin rummy."

"I am sort of hungry." I never did finish my breakfast.

"How does a grilled-cheese sandwich and tomato soup sound?" Mrs. Sweetwater got up from the table and motioned for me to sit across from Henry.

"That's my favorite lunch," I said.

"Sounds good to me," said Henry. He gathered the cards and put them in a little box on the counter. "What can I do to help?"

"Heat up the griddle," she said.

Henry and Mrs. Sweetwater worked as a team, buttering bread, opening cans, setting the table. I wondered if they were more than friends.

Henry left as soon as we'd cleaned up the dishes. We made ice-cream sundaes.

Mrs. Sweetwater ate a mouthful of whipped cream, and then pressed her hand on mine. "I want you to know that Henry and I are always here if you feel lonely and need to talk."

I didn't know what to say. I wondered if Mama told them we'd run away from home.

"Did you call my mama and tell her I wasn't going to school?"

"No. You were safe and sound, and I didn't want to upset her while she was at work. Figured there'd be time enough to let you talk to her when she got home."

"I acted like a baby."

"Nothing wrong with crying. I do it myself at least once a week. It clears the mind. Would you like to talk about what upset you?"

"I'm okay now." I wanted her to like me. If she knew the truth about us, she might change her mind.

Do you ever get confused, God? I heard that you love everyone, even the people who do bad things. I used to think that was strange, but now I understand. When I heard Daddy's voice, I couldn't help missing him. He told me he's stopped drinking. Is there some way you can let me know if he's telling the truth? Please, send me a sign. And thanks for Muriel and Henry. They're the best things about the Sweetwater Motel.

CHAPTER 18
Jailhouse Blues

MAMA DIDN'T have a hissy fit when I told her I'd called Daddy at work. We sat at the kitchen table eating rice pudding. Alice deserted us to watch TV.

"I know how hard it is to stop caring about him," she said. "It's taken me fifteen years."

"He said he's stopped drinking."

She tilted her head and sighed. "I wish I had a dollar for every time he's stopped drinking."

"He sounded okay. He didn't slur his words or anything."

Mama put down her coffee cup. "That's because he was at work. The real drinking starts the minute he gets home. Or on his way home when he stops off at a bar and has a few cold ones."

"Maybe he's learned his lesson this time."

"I doubt it."

"But this is the first time we left him. He said he misses us. He wants to change so we'll come back."

Mama pulled me onto her lap.

"Sarah Jane, this is not the first time I've run away from your daddy."

"But, Mama . . ."

"Hush now and listen. I left him twice when you were a baby. Before Alice was born. Both times he cried and told me he was sorry and he would never lay a hand on me again. I wanted to believe him because I still loved him and it wasn't easy being on my own with a baby."

"So you went back to him?"

"Yes, and it was good for a while. The social worker calls it the 'honeymoon period,' when everything seems perfect and lovey-dovey. What you need to understand is that nothing will ever change until he gets help. It's taken me this long to realize I can't help him. And neither can you."

"Maybe if he had his own service station again. That would make him happy."

"His problems started long before he lost his business. All the anger that comes out when he's drinking is always there right beneath the surface, even when he's sober. Nothing will ever make him happy. Not you, or me, or Alice, or a hundred service stations with his name on them. His ship is sinking, and if we go back, we will drown right along with him."

"Will he find us now? Because I called him?"

"Don't start fretting. Just don't do it again."

"If he finds us we'll have to run away and start over."

Mama folded her arms across her chest. "I'm done with running. If he comes after us and tries anything funny, I'll call the police. I didn't tell you because I didn't want you to worry, but I got a restraining order against him."

"What's a restraining order?"

"It's a piece of paper that says if your daddy comes anywhere near us, he'll be arrested."

"Do you want him to go to jail?"

"Any man who beats on a woman or a child

belongs in jail. I see that now. I should have pressed charges that night he hurt you, but I was afraid he'd get out on bail and kill the lot of us."

I tried to imagine what my daddy would look like in a prison uniform. "A real jail, with bars on the windows?"

Mama hugged me to her. "I know it seems mean, but what choice do I have? It's either put him someplace where he can't hurt us, or we'll be running and hiding for the rest of our lives." She turned my face to hers. "Is that what you want?"

"No, but I wish I could fix things so we could go home and be a family again."

"Well, that's not going to happen, so don't waste your wishes."

"Don't you believe wishes can come true?"

"Sure I do, but not that one. Wish for something practical, like a nice place for us to live."

I leaned my head against her chest. "I know Daddy hurt you, but I don't want him to go to jail." *And I don't want you to divorce him just yet,* I almost told her, but then she'd know I'd been snooping in her dresser, and I'd be grounded for life.

184

"Don't worry about something that might never happen. How about some good news for a change?"

"Okay." The only good news I wanted to hear was that we could move out of the motel.

"Did you know Henry works at a horse farm?"

"Yes, he told me he does barn chores."

"He could use some help. He'll pay you a fair wage and you can do some riding."

I jumped from her lap. "Did you ever think maybe I don't want to be around horses, seeing how I miss Pete real bad?"

"Don't take that tone of voice with me, young lady. Plenty of people are worse off than us. At least we have a roof over our heads."

"Oh, yeah, and it's such a nice roof. Who wouldn't want to live in a motel with moldy carpet and as a bonus get to clean up after slobs who leave snotty tissues on the floor?"

I ran into the bedroom, slammed the door and locked it. I didn't want to hear any more of her "good news."

"You have ten seconds to open that door." Mama rattled the knob.

Reluctantly, I unlocked the door. I lay down on the bed, my back to her. She closed the door and came to sit beside me.

"Don't you think I know this is hard for you? I'm homesick too." She stroked my hair.

"I miss Grandma Emma."

"Me too." Mama reached past me for the phone. "Let's give her a call."

"Can we really?"

"Why not?" Mama dialed her number and handed the phone to me. "You talk first, then I'll get Alice."

"Grandma, it's me, Sarah Jane."

I heard her give a little gasp as if she could not believe her ears. "Sweetheart, hearing your voice is the best thing that's happened to me in a month of Sundays. Are you all right? Are Alice and your mama with you?"

I filled her in on what we'd been up to for the past few weeks, and she gave me a report on Pete. I closed my eyes and pretended I was speaking to her from my house back home and she was just a few blocks away.

She made me promise to write to her and said

she'd send me funny cards and pictures of Pete. Alice pulled the phone away from me before I could tell her I missed her.

After Alice had her turn, Mama shooed us out of the bedroom. I listened from outside the door, and I could tell she was crying.

Later when she tucked me into bed I asked her if we'd ever see Grandma Emma again.

"Someday when it's safe," she said.

"Will I ever get to ride Pete again?"

"Someday."

I rolled over and buried my face in a pillow. My fingers found the holes in the bedspread. *Someday.*

Thanks for letting me talk to Grandma Emma last night. She said I could call her anytime and reverse the charges. She's going to send me some of my books. And she promised Alice a new doll. I'm going to write her a long letter as soon as I get home from school. She sounded lonely.

CHAPTER 19
Motel Girl

MAMA COOKED me pancakes the next morning. "How come you're still here? Won't you be late for work?"

"I've got new hours, so I don't have to be there until eight."

I poured a puddle of syrup. "Does that mean you can drive me to school?"

"No, it means I'll have an extra hour to myself in the morning. I'm not going to use it to drive you to school when you can take the bus."

The bus! I absolutely, positively couldn't take the bus. But how was I going to walk to school with Mama at home? She'd get suspicious if I left an hour early, but if I left at the regular time, I'd have to run all the way and I'd still be late.

I dressed slowly and pretended I forgot something at the last minute. If I missed the bus, she'd have to drive me to school.

She looked up from her second cup of coffee to check the clock. "Hurry up, Sarah Jane, or you'll miss the bus."

She was on to my plan. As soon as I had my stuff together, she hustled me out the door. I turned and waved to her, hoping she'd take pity on me and give in.

"Don't dawdle." She motioned for me to go.

I trudged the quarter mile up the road to the bus stop. Why had I eaten so many pancakes? They'd settled like rocks at the bottom of a pond.

I recognized Deena and Tracey among the kids who waited for the bus. Tracey looked me up and down. "What are you doing here?"

"This is my bus stop."

"Oh, really? Where do you live?"

"Down the street."

Deena looked in the direction I'd indicated. "There aren't any houses down there. Just the shopping center with the drugstore."

"It's behind some trees."

"You'll have to point it out as we go by."

Before they could continue the third degree, the bus pulled up. I rushed past them to get a seat. They plopped onto the seat in front of me.

I took deep breaths to calm myself and pretended to read a book. The bus slowed, then stopped behind traffic backed up at the light.

Tracey laughed and peered down at me from over the top of her seat. "Sarah Jane, I think someone is waving to you." She pointed outside the window.

There stood Mama, holding Alice aloft so she could see me on the bus. They stood near the road, their figures framed by the neon sign for the Sweetwater Motel. Alice waved her little arms and shouted my name. Even through the noise of the bus's engine, I could hear her loud and clear, and so could everyone else.

"What's wrong with you?" Fred asked me during homeroom.

"Nothing." How could Mama have been so stupid? If she wanted to make sure I caught the bus, did she have to stand in front of the sign with bigmouth Alice?

Tracey and Deena didn't come right out and ask me if I lived at the motel, but they spent the bus ride singing motel jingles.

"Are you going to tell me what's bugging you?" Fred had hold of the sleeve of my yellow sweatshirt. It was my favorite, and when I'd dressed for school that morning, I'd hoped it would bring me good luck.

"Later," I said and ran for gym. I changed into my gym uniform, and tossed my clothes into my locker.

We'd already gotten up to Rule Number Seven in Bosco's Rules of Life. "Silence is power." I think Mr. Bosco hoped that would keep us quiet in gym.

It was the first day of volleyball practice. We divided up into teams. Doug, Deena, and Tracey lined up on the opposite side of the net. Naturally I got Arthur on my team. He stood next to me in the middle row. I wondered if Tracey had already told everyone in gym about me living at a motel.

It was the most competitive practice I'd ever seen. Arthur apologized to me every time he missed a point, which was every time the ball came to him. He continued to get picked on whenever Mr. Bosco turned his back, but at least he'd stopped trying to protect me. Maybe that would stop the gossip about Arthur and me being in love.

After Mr. Bosco dismissed class, I stayed in the gym as long as I could, hoping Deena and Tracey would be dressed and gone by the time I got to the locker room.

No such luck. They stood next to my open locker, my clothes spilling onto the floor. I'd forgotten to lock it. As I walked toward them, Tracey turned her back to me and passed something to Deena, which she dropped into her purse. She slung the purse over her shoulder and nudged me with it accidentally-on-purpose as they left the locker room.

"Yikes, we're going to be late," said Tiffany, who dressed in slow motion.

I shoved my gym uniform into my locker, pulled on my jeans and my T-shirt, and yanked my sweatshirt over my head. "See ya," I called over my shoulder.

"Sarah Jane!" Tiffany called after me.

"Tell me later," I said and ran for class.

I heard some snickering as I walked to my desk. I figured it was just Doug and the rest of the jerks hoping I'd get into trouble for being late.

I'd been so preoccupied worrying about Tracey and Deena, that I almost forgot it was the day Mr. Tyrell would pair us off for our history projects.

Fred turned in her seat. "I hope we can be partners. My mom said we could meet at my house."

"Sounds good to me." It would be a relief if we could meet anywhere but the motel.

Mr. Tyrell cleared his throat. "I want you to work on your history project in groups of three. Diversity is the key to an interesting project."

He posted a sign-up sheet on the bulletin board and told us we had until Thanksgiving break to complete the project.

"Who should we ask to be in our group?"

Fred looked around the room, but it seemed as if everyone else had already formed groups.

"We'll be okay," Fred said to Mr. Tyrell. "Sarah Jane and I can do the project by ourselves. It'll be a piece of cake."

Mr. Tyrell didn't look convinced. "I think the projects are more interesting if there are at least three."

He furrowed his brow and glanced around the room, squinting, deep in thought, as if he were trying to come up with a plan for world peace. Arthur Proctor slinked into the room and handed him a late pass.

"I had a doctor's appointment," explained Arthur.

"Yeah, Arthur was at the pimple doctor," Doug said, and pretended to squeeze a zit.

"That's enough, Douglas. Settle down or you can stay after." Mr. Tyrell smiled at Fred and me. "Well, now, your problem is solved."

Fred and I gave him our best puzzled looks, knowing what he meant, but hoping it wasn't true.

"Arthur will be your third person." Mr. Tyrell returned to his desk, ending the discussion.

Mr. Tyrell spent the class time discussing possible subjects for our projects. Deena and Tracey announced that they would do their report on Cleopatra. Leave it to them to want to write about someone who wore lots of makeup.

The bell rang. Only one more period until lunch. Four more hours and I could go home. Maybe the worst was over.

As I walked past Arthur, he took hold of my wrist. "Sarah Jane, can I talk to you for a minute?"

"Not now, Arthur. We can talk about our project later."

"It's really important," he called after me.

I ignored him and dashed past Fred in the hall. "I'll see you at lunch," I called to her.

"Cheese and crackers!" she yelled. "Who did that to you?"

"Did what?"

Fred shoved me into the girls' room. She grabbed hold of my arms and spun me around with my back to the mirror.

"Look," she said, holding me in place, motioning with her head toward the mirror.

Even backward, I could read the words. Someone had scrawled MOTEL GIRL in black marker across the back of my yellow sweatshirt.

The room tilted, and I grabbed for the edge of the sink. My stomach churned and my breakfast rose in my throat.

I threw up in the sink. Chunks of pancakes, mixed with orange juice. It wasn't pretty and it smelled gross. My throat burned.

"Are you okay?" Fred passed me a wet paper towel. She tried to rinse out the sink, but the pancakes clogged the drain.

Tracey came into the bathroom with Deena. "What is that smell?"

"Maybe it's your breath," said Fred.

They peered into the sink. "That is so disgusting," said Deena.

Tracey stared at me. "Oh, nasty. You have barf on your face."

Deena shook her head. "Why didn't you hurl in the toilet? How is anyone supposed to use this bathroom?"

Fred placed herself between Deena and me. "This isn't the only bathroom in the building."

"Well, someone has to clean it up." Tracey sprayed perfume from a flask.

"I'll tell the custodian," said Fred.

"Maybe she should do it herself." Deena reached into her purse. "By the way, Sarah Jane, I like your sweatshirt. You'll have to tell me where you bought it."

Fred lunged at Deena. Deena jumped back, slamming her purse against the sink. It fell open. A hairbrush, lipsticks, a small mirror, and a black marker landed on the floor. The marker rolled and came to a stop at my feet.

I picked up the marker and held it behind my back. I was positive it was the same one Tracey had passed to Deena in the locker room.

I removed the cap. "Tracey, you have something on your face."

"I do?" She peered into the mirror long enough for me to reach around her and draw a mustache over her lip.

"Stop it!" She scrubbed at the mustache, which made it worse. It smeared into a fuzzy caterpillar.

Deena gasped. "You are dead meat." She

looked at Fred. "Both of you. Motel Girl and Mini-Me."

I rushed toward her, the marker aimed at her face. "How would you like a beard?"

I managed to get a few strokes of color on her chin before she ran from the girls' room, not bothering to wait for Tracey. Fred bared her teeth at Tracey, who gathered up her things and ran.

"Nice work. I didn't know you were so artistic," said Fred.

"There are lots of things you don't know about me."

"Like what?"

"I live at a motel."

"I sort of guessed that from the ad on your shirt."

"We have to live there because we don't have anywhere else to go."

"That sucks."

The second bell rang. "You'd better get to class."

"What are you going to do?"

"Go home before anyone else sees this." I pointed to my back.

"Don't let them win. You have as much right to be here as those cretins. I've had to put up with those two since kindergarten. They used to put my hat and mittens on a high shelf so I'd always be the last one ready to go outside."

"Did you tell the teacher?"

"No, I just learned to use the step stool. Come on, Sarah J. Wear your sweatshirt inside out."

"It won't work. It's got a hood."

"Are you naked under there?"

"No, I have a T-shirt on. But it's got a spaghetti-sauce stain on the front."

Fred yanked my sweatshirt over my head and stuffed it into my backpack. "There. You look fine. We'd better get going."

Maybe Fred was right. If I went home, I'd be letting them win. I remembered what Mama'd said. It was time to stop running.

Arthur waited outside the girls' room. He didn't say anything, just offered me his soft blue sweater to wear.

God, I wish I could take out a restraining order against Tracey and Deena. They are going to make my life miserable. I'm probably not supposed to use prayers to make bad things happen to people, but is it too much to ask for them to have diarrhea for a few days so Fred and I can have some peace?

CHAPTER 20

I Bury My Shirt

I TOLD HENRY I didn't feel well, and he said I could help out at the barn another day. Mama and Alice were still at the daycare center, so I had our place to myself. I stood by the open refrigerator drinking milk straight from the carton.

As I wiped my mouth on my sleeve, I realized I was still wearing Arthur's sweater. I took it off, then remembered my sweatshirt. I unzipped my backpack and pulled it out. Marion and I had bought two of them the last time we went shopping together back home. We planned to wear them to school on color day with our jeans, because our school colors were yellow and blue.

I stared at the words Motel Girl until they blurred.

I kissed my beautiful sweatshirt good-bye, rolled it into a ball, and stuffed it into the garbage pail under the sink. In between, doing my home-work, feeding Mabel, and starting dinner, I went back to the sweatshirt again and again, touching it one more time.

Fred called to make sure I was okay. During lunch I'd told her the truth about how we'd ended up at the motel, including all the gory details about Daddy. After I'd finished spilling my guts, she didn't say a word, simply got up from the table and bought me two ice creams with her own money.

Mama and Alice rolled in the door just as I hung up the phone. The oven timer beeped. I'd made frozen pizza, tossed salad, and carrot sticks.

"It is so nice to come home to dinner on the table." Mama hugged me, and then pulled a chair over to the sink so Alice could wash her hands.

She didn't ask me about the barn, so I didn't mention that I hadn't gone. Mama did that a lot lately. Forgot to ask about things, as if she had so many things on her mind, she couldn't take on one more thought. I didn't add to her burden by yelling at her for standing in front of the motel with Alice.

After dinner, I volunteered to give Alice her bath. It got me out of cleanup. I read the usual book to Alice and tucked her in with her blankie and a cup of water on the bedside table.

"I'm going to take a shower and turn in early," said Mama. "Don't stay up too late reading."

"I'm going to get a snack. You want something?"

"No, if I eat any more, I won't sleep."

Mama'd left on the soft light over the stove. I reached up into the cabinet above the sink and felt for the bag of cookies that I'd hidden behind the flour. The cellophane bag slipped from my hand and landed in the sink.

"Yuck." The sink was filled with sudsy water. I pulled out the bag of cookies. No damage done— to the cookies at least. My yellow sweatshirt, the one I had thrown away, floated in the water.

I plucked it out, quickly, as if it were a drowning person, then stood in the middle of the kitchen holding it by my fingertips, water drip-ping and spattering on the linoleum.

"What are you doing?" Mama came in wear-ing a bathrobe, a towel wrapped turban-style on her head. "Sarah Jane, do you hear me? You're flooding the kitchen."

"Why are you washing my shirt? I threw it away."

"But it's brand new." She unwound the towel from her head and draped it over a chair.

"Didn't you see what they wrote on it?" I held it open, the words even brighter now that it was wet.

"I'm sorry. I know how much you liked that shirt. I'll get it out."

I shook it at her, splashing her face in the process. "Don't you get it? They wrote MOTEL GIRL in permanent ink. It will never come out. I will always be Motel Girl. For as long as I live."

"Sweetie, when we have some extra money, we'll buy you a new one."

Did she really think buying a new shirt would erase everything that happened?

"We will never have extra money. We will never move out of this place. So stop making promises you can't keep."

"I never promised you this would be easy. I'm doing the best I can. All I'm asking is for you to be patient a little longer. I know how mean kids can be. Try to ignore them."

"I do try."

"Try a little harder. Once they get the message you don't give a darn about them, they'll leave you alone and pick on someone else."

I kicked at the cabinet door. "It isn't fair that we have to live here and Daddy gets to stay in our nice house."

"Sarah Jane, life is not meant to be fair. But you'll see. Try hard to make the best of things and pretty soon it will be easier."

I opened the cabinet door and slammed it shut. "You're not listening to me. You don't have to face those kids every day. The mean ones call me names and the nice ones pity me. And stop telling me to try harder. Why didn't you try harder to make things work out with Daddy? Couldn't you have done something to make him happy?"

"I don't need you telling me how to live my life. I did the best I could to keep this family together."

"Oh, yeah. Well, your best isn't good enough."

"Okay, Miss Know-it-all. What do you think

we should do? Maybe check into a penthouse suite at a fancy hotel?"

"Maybe we should go home. Daddy said he's stopped drinking and he's had plenty of time to cool down. He misses us real bad. I bet he'll be so happy to see us, he'll never be mean again."

"Your daddy will say anything to get us back. He's lying to you."

"You lied too. You told me we'd be living in our own apartment. And why did you have to stand in front of the motel with Alice when the bus went by? I hate living at this motel. I hate cleaning up after people and never being able to buy lunch at school or get a new shirt even when someone writes all over my favorite one. I hate you."

I shoved my yellow sweatshirt back into the garbage pail, then dumped the coffee grounds from Mama's leftover coffee on top and slammed the pail shut.

It didn't matter to me if I had hurt her feelings. She didn't have to go to school and face those kids. She didn't know how it felt to be a loser. To be Motel Girl.

Now I've gone and done it, God. Got Mama on my bad side. Enough said.

CHAPTER 21

I Make Plans

ALICE SHOOK me awake the next morning. "Mama says to get out of bed and get ready for school."

By the time I used the bathroom, they'd left. Mama'd left a note taped to the refrigerator that read *Take the bus to school.*

I figured she couldn't get any angrier with me, and she wasn't on my favorite-people list, so I dialed Daddy's number at home. He was probably at work, but I wanted to call anyway, to tell him I missed him.

The machine picked up.

"It's me, Daddy, Sarah Jane. I wanted to see if you're okay."

"Don't hang up." Daddy came on the line.

"How come you're not at work?"

"I started working third shift yesterday, so I was sleeping."

"Sorry. Go back to sleep."

"No, it's okay. Everything all right with you?"

"I want to come home." There, I said it. I'd been feeling it in my heart for a long time.

"Tell me where you are. I'll come get you."

"But you have to work."

"I've got some vacation time coming to me."

"I don't know, Daddy. Mama's got a restraining order against you. If I tell you where we are and you come to get me, the police will put you in jail."

I heard him sigh, long and hard. "Now, why did she go and do that? Did you tell her I stopped drinking?"

"Yes, Daddy, I told her about you changing, but she says you're lying. She says you'll say anything to get us to come home."

"It's different this time. You believe me, don't you, Sarah Jane? Please say you do or I swear to God, I might as well not go on living."

I wanted to believe him more than I ever wanted to believe anything. I couldn't bear the sadness in his voice. "Yes, Daddy, I believe you," I said, but something tugged at my heart. I couldn't be sure if it was love or doubt.

"Sarah Jane, you and me have to convince your mama that things will be better this time. But I can't do it from here. Tell me where you are and we can surprise her. That way she won't have time to call the police."

I glanced at the clock. "I've got to go or I'll miss the bus."

"Quick, tell me where you are."

"I have to go, Daddy." I hung up the phone.

All the way to the bus stop, I wondered if I'd made a mistake telling him about the restraining order, if warning him might have set something in motion that I'd be sorry for later.

Deena and Tracey got to the stop just as the bus pulled up. I let them get on first. It would have been a bad idea to let them get behind me, out of my sight.

As we passed the motel, Tracey stood up, and

like one of those tour directors, announced, "On your left, we are passing the Sweetwater Motel, home of Motel Girl, Sarah Jane Otis, and her family."

Every kid riding the bus craned his neck to stare at me, the way people gawk at an accident as they drive by.

I'll come get you and bring you home. That's what Daddy had said. All I had to do was call him and tell him where to find us and I'd never have to ride that bus again.

Fred and I hung out at her house after school. We had the place to ourselves, except for her older sister, who stayed in her room the whole time playing music loud enough for us to hear downstairs.

"I want to go home," I blurted out as soon as Fred and I sat down on the couch in her family room.

"You just got here. I thought we were going to watch a movie and start our history project."

"No, I mean I want to really go home, back to Georgia."

Fred tapped my forehead. "Have you lost all your brain cells? You said your father beat you and your mom."

"He hit me just the one time." I touched the scar on my cheek.

"You said he beat up your mom lots of times. That's why she left him."

"She hated what he did to her, but I think she finally left because he hit me."

"What if you go back and he hurts you again?" Fred clicked off the movie.

"He won't." But what if he did? I wouldn't have Mama to protect me, to fight him off with a kitchen chair, or a toaster or whatever else she got in her hands. "I'm so homesick, most days I don't want to get out of bed."

"Hey, Sarah J., you've got me." Fred took a bow.

"I know."

She smiled and rolled her eyes. "And you've got Arthur. By the way, he's coming by to work on our history project. It's due in two weeks."

My daddy would have called him a sissy for the way he let Doug and the other boys bully

him. But my daddy would have been wrong.
I'd come to realize there was a dignity to being
true to oneself even if it meant you'd never be
popular.

"I'll be gone by then." The words burst from
my mouth.

"Hold that thought." Fred went to the
kitchen and returned with a bag of chips and a
few cans of pop. "Okay, tell me what you're
scheming to do."

"I've been talking to my daddy on the
phone."

"Are you nuts? How can you trust him?"

"I have to, it's my last chance to get my family back together. He told me he's stopped drinking."

"What about me? Who's going to want to eat
lunch with weird little old me?"

I smiled at her. "You are weird, but not
because you're small. Don't you think it's strange
that you live in a really nice house, have lots of
clothes, plenty of spending money, but you still
steal things?"

"It's not like I'm a career criminal. I can stop

anytime I want to. I haven't stolen a thing in over
a week."

I grabbed hold of her hand. "You haven't?"

She tilted her head and widened her eyes.
"You know, I took most of the stuff for you. So
don't act all righteous."

"I know, but don't do it anymore, okay?"
Fred was right about me being guilty too. Guilty
for eating the food she took and for wearing the
clothes she stole. But what shamed me the most
was the way I'd used Fred. I'd been so consumed
with self-pity that I didn't care if she got caught.
All I cared about was easing my pain with things.
The way my daddy did with drink.

Fred snapped her fingers. "Earth to Sarah J.
If your dad can't come here and your mom won't
leave Ohio, it's going to be hard to arrange a family reunion."

The doorbell rang. Fred returned with
Arthur in tow.

"Hey, Sarah J." Arthur sat on the chair opposite me, a notebook on his lap.

Fred handed him a can of pop.

"Hey, Arthur." I wished he'd leave, so Fred

and I could figure out how to get my parents together. "I'll bring your sweater to school tomorrow."

"No hurry. So have you two come up with a plan?"

Fred and I stared at him.

"For the project." Arthur opened his pop. *Psshhhhh.* The hissing sound raised the hairs on the back of my neck.

Psshhhh. That familiar sound transported me back home, to those months before we left. I pictured Daddy sitting in his favorite chair, a six-pack of sixteen-ounce beers on the floor beside him. Some days he'd open one can after another, drink himself into a foul mood, and terrorize us until he passed out drunk. *Psshhhhh. Psshhhhh. Psshhhhh. Psshhhhh.*

Fred crushed the empty potato-chip bag. "Forget the history project. We've got something more important to do. Let's call it Project Sarah J."

Arthur laughed and stretched out his long legs. "What are you talking about? Are we giving her a makeover?"

I gave Fred a warning look. *Don't tell Arthur.*

"Do you want to go home or don't you?" Fred offered me a stick of gum.

"Yes, but . . ."

"Well, Arthur won't tell anyone your secrets and he might be able to help us come up with a plan."

Arthur nodded to me and crossed his heart. "You can trust me. Besides, who am I going to tell? The birds?"

Fred and I brought him up to date on my family history. At first he sided with Fred and said I was asking for trouble by returning to Georgia, but he came around when I told him I really believed my daddy had learned his lesson.

Arthur wrote all the facts in his notebook. He listed positives on one side and negatives on the other. Under negatives he wrote, *Fred and Arthur will be stuck with each other.*

Fred punched him in the arm. "I suppose this means I'll have to let you sit with me at lunch?"

"Or you could help me feed the birds," he said. "By the way, they prefer whole-wheat bread crumbs."

Fred sighed. "See what your leaving will do to

me? I may never forgive you." She offered Arthur part of her chocolate bar.

Arthur ate the chocolate, his brow furrowed, deep in thought. "What we have is a stalemate. Your mom won't go back to Georgia, and if your dad comes here, he'll end up in jail."

Fred tottered along the top of the couch, her arms outstretched, using its edge as a balance beam.

She dismounted, crashing to the floor. "I've got it. You don't need your mom or your dad. You can go back to Georgia on your own."

"Even if I can get there, Mama and Alice will be here."

"So you'll still have only half a family," said Fred.

Arthur held his pencil in the air. "Unless."

"Unless what?" I waited as he scribbled again in his notebook.

"Didn't you say that your mom finally left your dad because he hit you?"

"Yes, she left to protect me. And Alice." As soon as I said the words, I knew we'd found the answer.

Fred sat next to me. "What are you thinking?

"I'm thinking that if Mama left to protect me, then she'll go back to Georgia for the same reason. I just have to figure out a way to get myself there."

Fred pressed her lips together in concentration. "You could take a plane."

"Too expensive and besides, I don't like to fly."

Arthur kept scribbling, looking up from time to time to give me a reassuring smile.

"I know," said Fred. "A bus. It's cheaper than flying and you never leave the ground."

Arthur jumped up and strode across the room to the desk. "Is it okay if I use your computer?"

"Sure." Fred motioned for me to join her. We looked over Arthur's shoulder as he searched the Net for bus schedules.

He turned to me. "When do you want to leave?"

Please God, do not be mad at me for running away to Georgia, but this might be the last chance to reunite my family. Not to mention get us out of the motel. I know how busy you are, so I'm taking matters into my own hands and giving you one less thing on your To Do list.

CHAPTER 22
A Horse Named Pearl

I SPENT SATURDAY morning under a blanket on the couch watching a *Brady Bunch* rerun marathon. Seeing Marcia, Jan, and Cindy baking cookies with Mrs. Brady in their perfect kitchen did not cheer me up.

Arthur had reserved a ticket on a bus leaving the next Friday. I hid the computer reservation in my suitcase. Even with the tips I'd saved and the mad money from Mrs. Sweetwater, I was still twenty dollars short.

"I'm not going to eat a bite of food until you say I can get homeschooled," I told Mama. I could not go back to school, even if it was for just one more week.

"Suit yourself." She placed a tray on the coffee table. The grilled-cheese sandwich and tomato soup made my mouth water.

She said I could have the morning off from helping with the motel laundry, which got Alice riled up. "Leave Sister in peace," Mama told her before picking her up and carting her out the door.

I napped while they were gone. I'd been sleeping more and more. Some nights I went to bed before Alice. Mama said I was trying to escape from the real world.

"Wake up, Sarah Jane." Alice jumped up and down on the couch.

"Cut it out before you fall on me and knock out my teeth." I sat up and rubbed my eyes.

"Henry's here," she said.

Henry sat in the kitchen with Mama drinking coffee. She'd given him the last piece of chocolate cake.

"Hello, sleepyhead." She pulled out a chair for me.

"I didn't hear you come in." I smiled at Henry.

Mama topped off her mug from the coffee-pot. "That's because you wrap yourself in that quilt. It's a wonder you don't smother."

Henry put down his fork. "Are you ready to go to the barn?"

I'd forgotten about helping Henry with the chores. I gave out a big yawn.

"Maybe this isn't a good day." Henry placed his dishes in the sink and turned on the water.

"Leave those be, Henry. You and Sarah Jane get going before those horses wonder where you are." She gave me a look that said I'd better cooperate.

"I have to find my boots," I said.

"Hurry up. Henry's been waiting on you long enough."

Henry told Mama he'd take good care of me and gave Alice a piece of gum to make her happy. Ordinarily she didn't like to be left out, but she was scared of horses.

"Glad to see you wore your boots," said Henry.

We passed a sign that read BUCKEYE FARM. He turned his truck onto a long driveway bordered by fenced pastures. A mare and her foal grazed, side by side.

The driveway ended in a Y, with a white-shingled house to the left and a large barn to the right.

We parked in front of the barn. "Look around," said Henry. "I'll be back in a bit."

It took my eyes a minute to adjust to the shadows of the barn. I inhaled the syrupy scent of sweetfeed and the sharp smell of hay.

Beginning at one end of the aisle, I inspected each horse, stall by stall. I wondered which horse was Henry's.

"I see you're getting acquainted." A tall man wearing a plaid shirt and blue jeans stepped from the tack room, tipping his straw cowboy hat in my direction.

"Yes, sir. Is it okay?"

"It's fine with me, and the horses like the company. You must be Henry's friend Sarah Jane."

"Yes sir, Sarah Jane Otis."

"I'm pleased to meet you. My name's Tom."

He shook hands real nice, and he had a good

face, a face that said, *I will never tell you a lie.*

"Henry asked me to get you started mucking the stalls while he finishes watering the horses in the pasture."

"Which horse is Henry's?"

"The last stall on the left. The quarter horse named Roy, after Roy Rogers. He's fifteen, but he still acts like a three-year-old."

My heart pulsed inside my chest when I saw Roy for the first time. With his sleek brown coat and black stripe along his back, he could have been Pete's brother.

"My grandma Emma has a horse just like him."

"You must ride all the time."

"Not anymore. Pete's back where we used to live."

Tom removed his hat and wiped his forehead with a handkerchief he removed from his back pocket. "Sarah Jane, you're welcome to ride here whenever you want."

"Thank you." I said it to be polite, but I didn't think it would be fair to Pete to ride a strange horse.

"Why don't you start by mucking Roy's stall? Wheelbarrow's over there."

I slid open the door to Roy's stall, easing myself inside. "Hey, Roy, it's me, Sarah Jane. I'm Henry's friend." I kept my voice soft.

As I gave him a gentle nudge so he'd move and I could finish mucking his stall, he rubbed his head against me. Just like Pete always did. Tears swamped my eyes. I swiped at them with the tail of my shirt.

"See what you made me do." I gave Roy a pat, slid his door closed, and moved on to the next stall.

Tom kept busy loading bales into the hayloft. He looked down at me. "When you're finished with the mucking, how about grooming Pearl?" He nodded in the direction of the stall across from Roy's.

Under a coat of dried mud, Pearl was white, but any resemblance to a beautiful gem ended there. Her red-rimmed piggy eyes with upside down Vs that wrinkled her brow caused her to look worried. I'd be worried too, if I looked like Pearl. She had to be the strangest-looking horse I'd ever laid eyes on.

"That's Pearl," he said. "She's not much to look at, but she's a good old girl. Do anything you ask her to. She rolled around in the mud this morning to keep the flies off, so she's a mess."

"What kind of horse is she?"

Tom laughed. "Oh, she's a little of this and a little of that. Pearl belonged to Henry's wife, Ethel. They never had any children, so Pearl was her baby."

"I didn't know Henry was married."

"He and Ethel were married for over forty years. They ran this place together. Ethel could muck a stall faster than anyone I knew. And she could ride like she was born on a horse."

I looked around the barn. "This was Henry's place?"

Tom climbed down from the loft. "He lived here until Ethel died, and then he sold it to me and my wife. I worked here summers when I was a kid. Henry and Ethel treated me like family. When I bought the place, I told him Roy and Pearl could live out their lives here."

"Is that why he works here, to pay for their board?"

"I'd never charge him a cent to take care of his horses. But he's a proud man and likes to pay his way."

It puzzled me why anyone would give up such a fine farm. And it was even more baffling why he'd moved from the farm into a motel.

I would have given anything if Mama, Alice, and I could buy a horse farm. After we settled in, we could bring Grandma Emma and Pete to live with us. I couldn't let myself think about something so impossible. I had a better chance of winning the lottery.

After mucking the stalls, I filled the water buckets. I was getting myself a cold drink of water from a hose when Tom tapped me on my shoulder.

"Pearl is waiting on you," he said.

I gathered a halter, lead line, brush, curry-comb, and a hoof-pick. Pearl had that *Choose me* look on her face, the one Arthur Proctor got as he waited patiently to be chosen for a team in gym.

Okay, Sarah Jane, I told myself. *Even a piggy-eyed horse needs attention.* I put her in the crossties. Fewer daylight hours had caused her white coat to thicken for the winter ahead. I slid my hand beneath its softness.

For such an ugly horse, Pearl sure had a beautiful disposition. She stood quietly as I brushed her and lifted each hoof as soon as I touched her leg. She stood square on all four legs instead of leaning her weight against me, the way some horses do when you pick their hooves. It was as if she was trying to have perfect manners to make up for her less-than-perfect looks.

Pearl stood a hand smaller than Grandma Emma's horse Pete, so it was easy for me to reach across her back and groom every inch of her. Henry returned just as I finished braiding her mane.

"I see you've met Pearl. Isn't she something?" he said as he stroked her nose.

"Yes, she reminds me of my friend Marion back home."

Henry laughed. "Are you telling me you've got a friend who looks like a horse?"

I pictured Marion in my mind with her plain face that turned radiant when she smiled. "No, she doesn't look like a horse. But she's gentle like Pearl, and whenever I was with Marion, I felt peaceful. And safe."

"That about describes Pearl. She's the most trustworthy horse I've ever known. How about a ride?" Henry waited, still holding Pearl's halter. "She likes to lead."

Pearl was a born line leader. With me astride Pearl and Henry on Roy, we rode along the trails behind the farm. I never had to touch the reins; Pearl knew where to turn and she got us back to the barn in time for her dinner.

After we'd cooled down Roy and Pearl and returned them to their stalls, Henry treated me to milk and homemade brownies Mrs. Sweetwater had sent along.

We sat in the shade of a buckeye tree. "Henry, how come you live in the motel? Don't you miss being here on the farm?"

"I know it must seem strange to people, but living in one room at the motel is less lonely than rattling around in that big house by myself. I stayed on for a while after my wife Ethel died, but it got so every time I walked into the kitchen or looked out at the garden, I expected to see her there. It got to be too sad for me to live here alone."

"But it was your home."

"No, Sarah Jane, that's where you're wrong. A house is just bricks and timbers. Ethel was my home, and when she died, I felt lost."

"Do you like living at the motel?"

"What's not to like? I've got a nice room, work to keep me busy, and Muriel's good company."

Muriel was good company. So was Henry. I'd miss them both. "Do you want me to give the horses their grain?"

Henry looked at his watch. "Feed Pearl first. That's how Ethel did it."

Pearl nuzzled me as I said good-bye. I stroked her forelock. "Another day, Pearl, I'll ride you again another day."

The worried look reappeared in her eyes. She knew she'd never see me again.

Henry paid me twelve dollars, God. I can put it toward paying for my bus ticket. It felt good to be around horses. Give them some attention, good hay, and cool water, and they like you no matter what you look like or what you wear. And they couldn't care less where you live.

CHAPTER 23

By Myself Alone

O N SUNDAY night, I begged, pleaded, and cried to Mama to let me stay home the next day. I pretended to be sick, making my voice raspy so she'd think I had a sore throat.

At first she ignored me. When that didn't work she kept me occupied folding laundry, cleaning the litter box, giving Alice a bath.

I was still nattering at her when she turned out all the lights and went to bed on the pullout couch.

"You can stay up all night for all I care," she said to me in the dark, "but you are going to school tomorrow. And don't even think about turning on a light."

I sat alone in the dark kitchen, feeling sorry for myself. No one in the whole entire world could be more miserable than I was. I wished I could click my red boots together and be back in my house that very instant.

Padding across the living room, I slid my hand into Mama's purse and took all her change. I let myself out and walked to the pay phone set next to the ice machine.

The operator told me how much to deposit. The coins made a loud noise.

Daddy answered the phone.

"Hello," I said softly, afraid someone might hear and come to see what I was doing.

"Who is this?" Daddy sounded funny, as if I'd woken him from a sound sleep.

"It's me, Sarah Jane."

"Is your mama there?"

"She's sleeping."

"You all right?"

"I want to come home, Daddy." I tried hard not to cry, but a sob caught in my throat.

"Tell me where you are."

"No, Daddy, you can't come get me. You'll

end up in jail. But I have a plan. A good one."

I almost ran out of money before I could give him all the information. He promised to pick me up at the bus station. "I'll be there with bells on," was what he had said.

Mama snored on as I slipped through our door. In the bedroom, Alice lay on her side, her blankie scrunched to her chest. After Friday, who knew when I might see her again? I curled up next to her, still in my clothes. I didn't want to sleep alone, even if it meant getting kicked all night by my little sister.

It might be my imagination run wild, God, but every time I look up from what I'm doing, I see Mama watching me. And Alice has taken to following me around, as close as a car riding my bumper. They remind me of a dog we used to have who always knew when you were getting ready to leave.

CHAPTER 24

Signs

MAMA STOOD her ground and sent me off to school on Monday. Every time Tracey or Deena said something nasty, I reminded myself that Friday was the last day I'd have to see their ugly faces.

Fred, Arthur, and I ate lunch together every day, using the time to finalize my plans.

"My mom is going to call your mom tonight to tell her my sister will pick us up at school on Friday and drop us off in town to do some shopping," said Fred. "My mom never gets home from work until six, so she won't be a problem."

Arthur entered the information into the "SJ" notebook. "Okay, here's the schedule. You take the four o'clock bus into Columbus. That will give you plenty of time to make the six-fifteen bus to Georgia."

"And I'll give you one of my sister's shirts and a pair of her earrings to make you look older." Fred undid my ponytail and fluffed my hair. "Definitely wear your hair down."

Arthur read from the computer printout. "Yeah, it says you have to be fifteen to travel alone at night, so wear lots of makeup."

"What if they won't let me on the bus?"

Fred shook a finger at Arthur. "Quit giving her something else to worry about." She turned to me. "Do like we did at the movies and wait until the bus driver's busy helping a little old lady with her bags, hand him your ticket, and boogie to the back of the bus. Lay low until you get to Georgia."

"I think I might have to pee sometime."

"There's a bathroom on the bus," said Arthur.

"And I'll pack you a snack so you won't have to get off the bus at all. The less the driver sees you, the better."

Arthur nudged Fred. "Won't your mom call

Sarah Jane's mom if she's not here when she gets home from work?"

"I'm telling her Sarah J. got sick and her mom picked her up."

"Right, and Mama's not expecting me home until Saturday night. By the time she starts worrying about me, I'll be back home in Georgia."

Arthur pointed to the route my bus would take. "It's going to stop to pick up passengers at all these spots. That's why taking the bus is good, if you change your mind, you can get off."

"Why would I want to do that? I have to get home, Arthur. I'm not going to change my mind."

"Yeah, Arthur," said Fred. "Sarah J. is the most stubborn person I know. The girl has made up her mind."

By Thursday I had dark circles under my eyes from lack of sleep. Between worrying about Mama and Alice discovering my plans and feeling depressed about leaving them, my brain began to short-circuit.

Thank goodness for Fred. She thought like a

criminal and took care of the smallest details. And Arthur kept both of us calm.

One of the teachers at Little Lambs Daycare called in sick on Friday, so Mama had to go in early. I barely got to tell her good-bye.

She leaned down to kiss me as I lay in bed. "Don't forget to feed Mabel before you go to school."

"I won't forget." I sat up and gave her a tight hug.

She looked startled. "What's that for?"

"I won't see you until tomorrow night. Remember, I'm sleeping over at Fred's."

"I almost forgot. Have a good time and don't drive her mama crazy."

I wanted to give Alice a hug good-bye too, but that might tip off Mama that something was up. "See you later, Alice," I called to her from the open doorway; but she was already in the car.

Mabel brushed up against my legs as I packed to leave. I picked her up and kissed the top of her head. "Be a good cat," I told her, then gave her some food to keep her busy.

I put some clothes, the ticket information,

and a book to read on the bus into my backpack. The weather had turned cool, so I grabbed my jacket from the closet and filled the pockets with photos of Mama and Alice, two packs of gum, and a postcard of the Sweetwater Motel.

I planned to write a thank-you to Muriel and Henry the first chance I got. And to tell them I was sorry I didn't say good-bye.

Fred and Arthur insisted on escorting me to the bus station in Columbus. They helped me pay for my ticket and gave me an extra five dollars. We sat at a table eating hot dogs while we waited.

"Take this." Fred handed me a cell phone. "Don't worry, it's not stolen. My mom gave it to me for emergencies, and if this doesn't qualify as an emergency, I don't know what does."

I hesitated to take it.

She pushed it at me. "You can mail it back to me after you get there. My number is on speed dial just in case."

"Thank you." I slipped the phone into my pocket. "I almost forgot." I removed Arthur's blue sweater from my backpack.

"Keep it. It might be cold on the bus."

"I have a jacket."

"Keep it anyway. You can give it back to me the next time I see you."

Fred smiled. "Yeah, now that we know the bus schedule, we might surprise you one day."

Someone announced that the bus to Georgia was departing in five minutes.

"Okay," said Fred. "Let's check out the makeup." She applied another layer of lip gloss and a few sweeps of mascara, almost poking my eye out in the process.

"You look at least sixteen," said Arthur.

"Yeah," said Fred. "You're tall for your age and the boots make you look even taller. Maybe I should get myself a pair."

We bided our time until the bus driver got busy scrambling to ticket the passengers' luggage. I handed him my ticket, and he did his thing without ever looking up.

I wished Fred and Arthur could come along for the ride. I might have stood there forever if Fred hadn't given me a gentle shove.

"Go! Walk to the back of the bus and slump down in your seat."

"Pretend you're sleeping," said Arthur. "That way no one will bother you."

We did a group hug. "Hey," yelled Fred as I mounted the steps to the bus. "I'm number one on the speed dial."

I practically held my breath until I heard the whoosh of the door as it closed. We were on our way.

The bus headed south. It had grown dark by time we crossed the Ohio River. I looked down from my window seat; the lights from the bridge reflected off the water.

At eight o'clock, we stopped to take on passengers. Mama would be tucking Alice into bed and reading her a story.

By midnight we'd made two more stops and filled most of the seats. A lady wearing a purple raincoat and carrying a shopping bag sat next to me. She listened to music on her headphones. Alice would be sound asleep, dreaming of costume jewelry. I pictured Mama sitting up in bed reading a romance novel.

I was too excited to sleep. I checked the clock

on Fred's cell phone and counted the hours until I'd arrive in Georgia. Daddy would be waiting for me at the bus station. He had promised.

My feet ached, so I yanked off my boots. I dozed off sometime before dawn, using Arthur's blue sweater for a pillow. We stopped for breakfast in a small town in Tennessee.

I would have loved a stack of pancakes, but I was afraid that in the light of day, with my makeup worn off, the bus driver might call security or whoever they call when they catch an underage kid on the bus.

Most of the other passengers got off the bus and filed into the diner. A few came back with coffee and newspapers. I used the time to brush my teeth and slick on more lip gloss and some blush, just in case.

We pulled into the Macon bus station at lunchtime to drop off and pick up more passengers. We had a thirty-minute layover. All the food Fred had packed for me was gone. My stomach rumbled. I got off the bus and went into the bus station.

Pulling out my last five dollars, I ordered

a grilled-cheese sandwich. Daddy would still be at home. I finished my sandwich, wiped my hands, and pulled Fred's cell phone from my pocket.

The phone rang five times. The answering machine clicked on. "Daddy, it's me, Sarah Jane."

Someone picked up the phone. I heard a clunk as the phone hit against something.

"Hey there, Sarah Jane. Where are you? I thought you wouldn't be getting here for another hour."

"I'm in Macon, Daddy. We're stopped here for a bit."

"For a minute there, I thought I wrote the time down wrong."

"What are you doing?" I heard the sound of the TV in the background.

"Just sitting here in my recliner, relaxing. Saving my strength so we can have some fun when you get home."

"What are we going to do first?" Was that a slur in his voice or was he just tired?

"Hold on a minute." I heard him put down the phone. A minute later he came back on. "Sorry, what were you saying?"

I was about to ask him again what he had planned for us, but before I could speak, I heard it. That sound. *Psshhhh.*

It could have been a can of Coca-Cola, or a root beer, or any other kind of soda pop in the world. But there was that *ping* in my heart. Maybe it was the sign from God I'd been praying for, a warning that something was not right and I'd better listen.

I watched through the plate-glass window as the passengers reboarded the bus. The bus that would take me home, back to Daddy.

"I have to go, Daddy. The bus is about to leave."

"Okay, baby girl. I'll see you soon."

"I'll see you soon." I remained still, made no move to go to the bus, just watched as it pulled away from the station.

Daddy would be waiting for me. If I didn't get off the bus, he'd figure out that I'd changed my mind. He knew where I was, so it wouldn't be long before I'd see his Buick come flying into the parking lot.

I wanted to call Mama, but even if I did, by the time she got to Macon, I'd be long gone. This wasn't what I'd planned. I'd wanted to go home so badly that I'd run away from Mama, the one person who would lie down and die for me.

My last three dollars wouldn't get me far. Crazy thoughts of hiding someplace until Daddy gave up and left buzzed through my mind. But where?

An elderly lady walked up to the ticket counter. I heard her ask for a ticket to Atlanta. She reminded the ticket seller that she wanted the senior fare.

Grandma Emma always asked for senior fare when we went to the movies. Grandma Emma.

I dialed her number. *Please be home.* Her answering machine picked up.

"Grandma Emma, it's me, Sarah Jane." I didn't want her to hear me crying. I took a deep breath to calm myself. "I'm okay, but I've done something really stupid. I was coming home to see you and Daddy. Mama was right, he'll never change, but now I'm stuck at the bus station in Macon. Daddy knows I'm here and when I don't show up, he's going to come after me. Mama can't get to me in time and besides, she thinks

I'm at a sleepover at Fred's house. I probably don't sound as if I'm making any sense, but please come get me. If you do, I promise, I will never do anything like this again for the rest of my life." A sob caught in my throat. "Please come as fast as you can, but drive safely."

I didn't want to hang up the phone and break the connection, so I stayed on until I heard the answering machine's tape come to an end.

Grandma Emma could be anywhere. She might be at the movies or having lunch with a friend. Or maybe she was in the barn with Pete.

I spent a dollar on a bottle of pop and made myself comfortable on a chair in the ladies' room. If I hung out too long in the waiting room, someone might get nosy and wonder why I was by myself.

It crossed my mind to hide in one of the stalls so Daddy couldn't find me. But I wouldn't put it past him to barge in and drag me to the car.

I checked the time. Daddy would be on the highway, passing every car in sight, honking at the ones that wouldn't move over.

Beads of sweat covered my face and neck. I took off my jacket. A lady and two kids came in to use the toilets. The kids stared at me until the lady hurried them into a stall.

One more hour and he'd be here. Sooner, if he speeded. I closed my eyes and prayed.

God, it's me, Sarah Jane. I am praying to you from a ladies' room in a bus station in Macon, Georgia. If that was you who sent me the sign that my daddy hasn't changed, that ping *in my heart, thank you very much. It arrived too late, which is why I am in this predicament. I don't blame you. You've probably been sending me signs all along and I wasn't listening. I didn't listen to Mama either. She was right. Daddy will never change. The thing is, I want to go home, to Mama and Alice. Please help me. Amen.*

I had to leave the shelter of the ladies' room to use the cell phone. A police officer sat at the lunchroom counter. It would be so easy to go up to him and tell him my story. But what if Daddy showed up and sold him a pack of lies? Or if the policeman called social services and they put me in a foster home until the courts could straighten everything out?

I heard Mama's voice in my head telling me not to be a drama queen, but I couldn't take the chance of trusting him. I opened the door and stepped outside.

I tried Grandma Emma's number again. No answer. It would be mean to call Mama, scare her to death when she was so far away and couldn't do anything to help me.

Staring at the cell phone, I jabbed the speed dial. Number one for Fred.

"It's me, Sarah Jane."

Fred shrieked, "It's her," to someone in the room. "Arthur's here. We're working on the history project. Are you home? Are you with your dad?"

Before I could answer, I spied my daddy's Buick on the horizon. The car swerved to miss hitting someone crossing the road.

"I have to go. Call my mama and tell her I'm at a bus station in Macon, Georgia. Tell her I'm sorry I didn't believe her. Tell her I want to come home."

Please do not let him find me, God. I will read to Alice every night and never skip a page. And from now on I will try to be a better listener.

CHAPTER 25

Rule Number Seven

SLIPPING THE phone in my pocket, I hoisted my backpack over my shoulder and hid between two parked vans, squatting to make myself as small as possible.

I heard the screech of brakes and the slam of a car door. Peering under one of the vans, I spied Daddy's work boots, the ones spattered with red paint from the Chevy we fixed. Only the van stood between us.

He paused and I imagined him scanning the parking lot, looking for me. I waited for him to go inside the bus station. I'd have to make a run for it, find a better place to hide.

I saw another pair of feet. They stopped near

my daddy's. Daddy moved away. I breathed a sigh of relief until I heard someone open the van's door and heard the roar of its engine.

The van drove off leaving me exposed. Daddy was almost to the station. I froze in place, afraid to move, terrified that any movement might cause him to turn.

He paused at the entrance. His shoulders stiffened. Too late, I realized he'd seen my reflection in the plate-glass window.

Spinning on his heels, he turned and ran for me. He could have walked or crawled. It didn't matter. There was nowhere for me to run.

"What kind of game are you playing, Sarah Jane?" Even from a distance I heard the rage in his voice.

"I missed the bus, Daddy."

"Then why were you hiding from me?"

"I wasn't hiding. I was waiting for you. I figured you'd come get me when I didn't get off the bus back home."

"You know what I think," he said as he took hold of my wrist. "I think you're a liar just like your mama."

"No, Daddy, I'm telling you the truth."

His eyes narrowed. "Did you know your mama hired some hotshot lawyer to serve me with divorce papers?" The words spewed from his mouth, carrying alcohol fumes on his breath.

"I didn't know," I said, trying to keep him calm, to buy myself more time.

Why hadn't I trusted Mama? At that very moment she was probably cleaning the motel rooms, stripping sheets from the beds of strangers, doing everything she could to make us a better life.

Daddy pulled me closer, twisting my arm in the process. "I got the papers this morning. Some self-important process server comes to my door and shoves them in my hand." His lips twisted with rage. "Your mama didn't even have the decency to call and break the news herself. She lets some outsider tell me she wants a divorce."

He tightened his grip on my wrist, hard enough to turn his knuckles white. "Who does she think she is, taking my kids away from me? Well, now she'll know how it feels because she's going to have to come crawling back to me on her hands and knees if she ever wants to see you again."

He pulled me in the direction of his car. I dug in my heels, looking toward the bus station. The police officer I'd seen sitting at the lunch counter came outside, pausing by the door, observing us.

"Anything wrong?" he called.

I remained still, sending a silent message to the policeman with my eyes. I turned back to my daddy. He let go of my wrist. I felt a surge as the power moved from Daddy to me.

The policeman walked toward us.

"Everything's fine." Daddy told him. "Keep your mouth shut," he whispered to me, "or I'll tell him you ran away and I'm taking you home."

"Where you folks headed?" The police officer strolled over to us, his hand resting on his hip, close to his holstered gun.

Daddy got a grin on his face. "My little girl spent too much time in the ladies' room and missed her connection. I'm just picking her up. We're going to head home now."

"Is that what happened?" The police officer turned me gently away from my daddy.

This was my chance. *Tell him, Sarah Jane, let him know what's going on. Tell him you want to go home. Home to Mama and Alice.*

The officer had a kind face, clear blue eyes, and strong-looking hands. I wanted to trust him, but I was scared. What if he believed Daddy? What if Daddy convinced him I *was* a runaway?

"Yes, I missed my bus." That's what I'd told Fred that first day of school. Now I might never see her again. Why had I thought I'd be better off going home to Daddy?

The policeman placed his hand on my shoulder, saying nothing, giving me time to change my mind.

"We need to hit the road," said Daddy. "Beat the traffic."

"Okay folks, have a safe trip. I'm going to finish my lunch." The police officer removed his hand from my shoulder and in an instant my lifeline vanished.

Daddy moved toward me. "I'm hungry," I said.

"We'll get something on the road."

"I want to eat now." Before he could protest, I ran across the parking lot, close on the heels of the policeman.

I hunkered in a corner of a booth while Daddy ordered our food at the counter. The policeman turned from where he sat and smiled at me. I smiled back before dialing Grandma Emma's number one more time. Still no answer.

Daddy inhaled his chili dog and fries. He watched me as I chewed each bite of my grilled-cheese sandwich twenty times.

"Don't think I don't know what you're doing, Sarah Jane."

"I'm not doing anything, just eating my sandwich."

He leaned across the table. I saw my reflection in his eyes. "You can take all day and it won't make a bit of difference. Your mama can't help you now."

I dropped the rest of my grilled cheese on the plate. He was right. Even if Fred had managed to reach Mama, she'd never get to me on time. I gathered my things, all the while plotting on how to get away from Daddy the minute we got back home, before he could lock me in my room. I'd jump from the car and run through the woods to Grandma Emma's, take the same route Mama, Alice, and I did the night of the storm.

"Let's go." Daddy rose from his seat, jabbing the table with his finger. He moved slowly across the waiting room, his anger hidden from strangers. It revealed itself in his arms held close to his body, and in his hands, clenched into fists.

The police officer looked up from his dish of apple pie and ice cream to nod at me. I wiggled my fingers at him in reply.

Daddy opened the passenger door to his car. "Get in."

"No!" I said.

We stood a few feet apart, close enough for me to see the danger in his eyes, the same look I'd seen that night in our kitchen back home. The night he came after me.

His eyes focused on something behind me. I sensed without looking, could tell by the set of Daddy's jaw, that the police officer had come outside.

"Get in the car, Sarah Jane. Don't make me say it again."

"No." This time I said it in a whisper.

"This is your last chance. Get in the car or I'm telling that policeman you ran away from home. You know what they do to runaways, don't you?"

Rule Number Seven from Bosco's Rules of Life popped into my head. *Silence is power.* I remained mute and stroked the crescent-shaped scar on my cheek, the one my daddy had put there.

Without a word, he closed the door and moved to the driver's side. A car raced into the parking lot, coming to a halt a few feet from us. I couldn't believe my eyes. Grandma Emma!

I threw myself into her arms the instant she stepped from her car. "You came," I said. "I called you, but you weren't home. How did you know I was here?"

"I called home to check my messages. I would have called you back, but you didn't leave a number. So I jumped in my car and got here as fast as I could." She looked over at my daddy. "Looks like I got here in the nick of time."

"I've got my rights, Emma," said Daddy. "She's my daughter."

Grandma Emma hustled me into her car. "Not anymore. You lost your rights the day you beat her."

The police officer came over to ask about our change of plans. He stood outside Grandma Emma's open window. "You folks having a family spat?"

"No, officer, everything's hunky-dory. I'm Sarah Jane's grandma."

He looked over at my daddy. "Is this okay with you, sir?"

Daddy hesitated, as if he were trying to come up with a lie good enough to get me away from Grandma Emma. Something convincing to tell the policeman.

Sitting next to Grandma Emma and with the policeman right outside the car, Daddy didn't look so scary. He acted tough, but he was nothing but a bully.

I tapped my red boots against the car floor. "Let's go."

"We'll be on our way now, officer," said

Grandma Emma, staring at Daddy, daring him
to try and stop her.

I craned my neck to watch the scene we left
behind through the back window. The police
officer faced Daddy. He looked as if he were asking him questions. I wished I could hear Daddy's
answers.

Just as we crested the hill near the entrance to
the highway, a police cruiser, its siren wailing, its
lights flashing, passed us going in the direction of
the bus station.

Someone's in trouble, I thought, but I didn't
care. I was going home.

*Hello, God. Thanks for sending Grandma Emma.
She said right in the middle of her bingo game,
something told her to call home and check her messages. I figured it was you. We're staying at a motel
in Kentucky. This is as far as we got before it turned
dark. Grandma Emma doesn't like to drive at
night, so we'll leave for home first thing in the
morning. This is the first time I've thought of Ohio
as home. I realize now that home is the place where
I am loved and where I am safe. Home is where I
will hug Mama and Alice good night and sleep all
the way through till morning.*

CHAPTER 26
Homecoming

"DID YOU CALL Mama?" I asked Grandma Emma as soon as we got into our room at the Days Inn Motel.

"Didn't want to waste a minute. But we've got plenty of time now."

I held out the phone. "One day when I have a million dollars, I will give you every penny if you'll talk to her first."

She came to sit beside me on the bed. "Let's call her together."

Mama must have been sitting on the phone. She picked up at half a ring. She said she wanted to come and get me, but she knew she wouldn't get there on time. So she did the only thing she could. She called the police and told them her little girl was stranded at the Macon bus station.

"Did you tell them about Daddy?"

"You better believe I did. Gave them a description of his car and his license plate number, in case he took off with you before they got there."

I remembered the cruiser with the flashing lights. Daddy was going to have a lot of explaining to do.

We got on the road early the next morning. Grandma Emma let me play whatever I liked on the car radio. I took off my boots and massaged my toes.

"Are your tootsies sore?" Grandma Emma patted my foot.

"My feet must have grown. My boots don't fit me anymore."

"I'll buy you a new pair when we get to Ohio."

"Thanks." I'd polish my red boots real good when I got home, wrap them up, and give them to Fred. Even if they didn't fit her right away, she could wear them around her house.

As we drove along the bridge that crossed the Scioto River, I used Fred's cell phone one last time.

Alice picked up on the first ring. "It's Sarah Jane," she screamed.

Mama came on the line.

"We're almost home."

"Where are you?"

"We're heading over the bridge. Now we're passing the market. We're turning into the driveway. There's the motel sign." I let out a gasp.

"What's wrong, baby girl?"

I couldn't believe my eyes. Just beneath the words SWEETWATER MOTEL, the sign read WELCOME HOME, SARAH JANE.

Mama rushed to the car, Alice at her heels. Muriel and Henry watched from the office window.

I fell into Mama's arms. "Do you hate me? Do you hate me for going back to Daddy?"

She rubbed my back the way she used to when I had trouble falling asleep. "Hush now. How can I blame you for doing the same thing I did over and over? I'm just glad you're safe."

After dinner we cuddled on the couch, all four of us, including Grandma Emma. Mabel curled up on my lap.

"So, Sarah Jane, are you planning on taking another trip anytime soon?" Mama stroked my bangs back from my face.

I pressed closer to her. "Mr. Bosco, my gym teacher, teaches us Bosco's Rules of Life."

"You don't say."

"Yes, and from now on, Mama, I'm living my life according to Rule Number Two."

She smiled at me. "This, I have to hear."

I nuzzled my cheek into the crook of her neck. "'At the end of the day, go home.'"